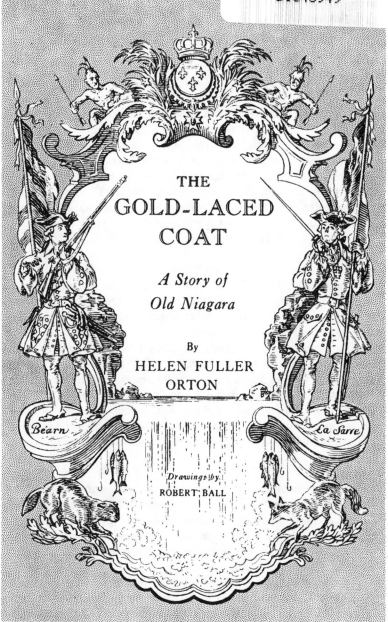

THE

# GOLD-LACED COAT

*A Story of*
*Old Niagara*

By

HELEN FULLER
ORTON

*Bearn*

*La Sarre*

*Drawings by*
ROBERT BALL

This publication is made possible by a major grant from the Ferguson Foundation, Buffalo, New York, by a gift from Mrs. Marion H. Anthony, by memorial gifts from the friends of William G. Fraize, and by individual gifts from the friends of Old Fort Niagara.

# PREFACE TO THE
# OLD FORT NIAGARA EDITION

Helen Fuller Orton's *The Gold-Laced Coat* is, without question, the best known and loved children's tale of the Niagara Frontier. From its first printing in 1934 the book went through fifteen editions, the last in 1961. Mrs. Orton's story of Philippe de Croix's adventures with his friends Pierre, Red Bird and Abbie Wentworth is both appealing and historically accurate. The novel has introduced several generations of elementary school students to the early history of the Niagara Frontier. On the basis of these merits, the Old Fort Niagara Publications Committee decided to reprint this classic novel for young people. The Old Fort Niagara edition has been printed from J.B. Lippincott's eighth impression, thus preserving the original type face and illustrations.

Set at Fort Niagara during the tumultuous years of the French and Indian War, *The Gold-Laced Coat* was carefully researched by its author. Mrs. Orton used the best secondary sources of her time as well as primary material to provide background for her story. These works are cited in her acknowledgements.

Particularly recommended for further reading are Frank H. Severance, *An Old Frontier of France* (1917), Pierre Pouchot, *Memoir on the Late War in North America* (1866 translation and edition by Franklin B. Hough) and Brian Leigh Dunnigan, *Siege 1759 - The Campaign Against Niagara* (1986). For concise overviews of the history and design of Fort Niagara see Dunnigan, *A History and Guide to Old Fort Niagara* and *History and Development of Old Fort Niagara* (both 1985).

Reprinting of *The Gold-Laced Coat* would not have been possible without the assistance and cooperation of a number of people. Particular thanks to the Orton family for generously consenting to the project and to Douglas T. Orton for expediting the process. Thanks also to the Harper & Row Company for granting permission to reproduce the earlier edition. The cheerful cooperation of Nancy Gallt is greatly appreciated.

Financial support for this project was provided by the Ferguson Foundation, by Mrs. Marion H. Anthony, by the friends of the late William G. Fraize, and by individuals, notably Ray Wigle and Rev. William Amann in the name of Sr. Anne Brennan, who grew up with the story of Philippe's gold-laced coat.

# The GOLD-LACED COAT

## BOOKS BY HELEN FULLER ORTON

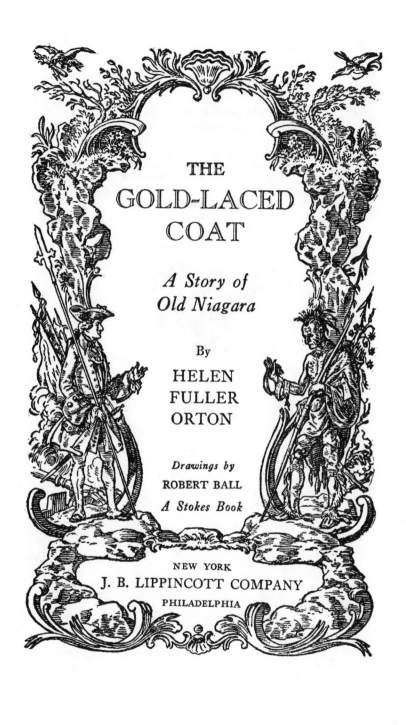

# THE
# GOLD-LACED
# COAT

*A Story of
Old Niagara*

By

HELEN
FULLER
ORTON

*Drawings by*
ROBERT BALL

*A Stokes Book*

NEW YORK
J. B. LIPPINCOTT COMPANY
PHILADELPHIA

# ACKNOWLEDGMENTS

ACKNOWLEDGMENT is gratefully given, for help received, to Mr. R. W. G. Vail, of the American Antiquarian Society (Worcester, Mass.), who read the manuscript and gave valuable criticism; to Dr. Arthur C. Parker, Director of the Rochester Museum of Arts and Sciences, an authority on Iroquois customs, who cleared up obscure points; to Colonel C. H. Morrow, 28th Infantry, Post Commander of Fort Niagara, who encouraged me in the undertaking, read the manuscript and gave valuable information; to Mr. A. H. Hooker, of Niagara Falls, who gave important data concerning the old Portage and loaned me rare maps and books; to Mr. Claud H. Hultzén, Executive Vice-

ACKNOWLEDGMENTS

President of the Old Fort Niagara Association, who furnished interesting details of the Fort in the French period; to Mr. Denton A. Fuller, Jr., of Buffalo, who loaned me valuable books and gave important information; and to Mr. Victor Hugo Paltsits and the staff of the American History Department of the New York Public Library, who most courteously assisted in the use of the facilities of the library.

For kind permission to use the two maps from "An Old Frontier of France," my thanks are extended to Mrs. Frank H. Severance, of Buffalo.

For the historical facts, I am chiefly indebted to that scholarly work, "An Old Frontier of France," by Dr. Frank H. Severance; to "Memoirs of the Late War in America," by Captain François Pouchot, last French Commandant of Fort Niagara; to "The Story of the Old Stone Chimney," by Peter A. Porter; to "The Diary of Sir William Johnson," and to "Documents Relative to the Colonial History of the State of New York."

HELEN FULLER ORTON.

# CONTENTS

# CONTENTS

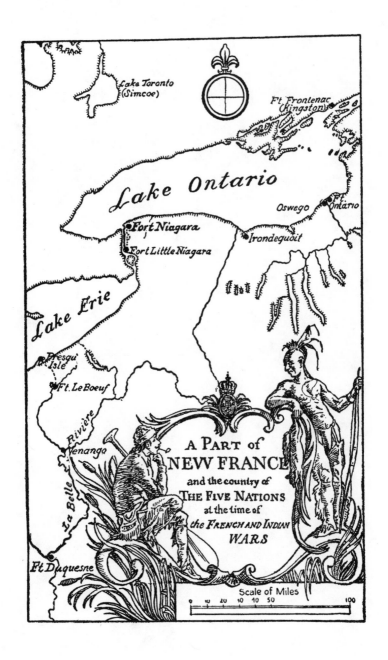

Lake Toronto
(Simcoe)

Ft. Frontenac
(Kingston)

Lake Ontario

Oswego

Ft. Ontario

Fort Niagara

Irondequoit

Fort Little Niagara

Lake Erie

Presqu' Isle

Ft. Le Boeuf

Rivière

Venango

La Belle

A PART of
NEW FRANCE
and the country of
THE FIVE NATIONS
at the time of
the FRENCH AND INDIAN
WARS

Ft. Duquesne

Scale of Miles

0    10    20    30    40    50                    100

# THE GOLD-LACED COAT

## CHAPTER I

### THE BOY FROM FRANCE

"WAKE UP, Philippe, wake up! Here is a fine day!" It was the voice of Pierre, the voyageur.

Philippe, a lad of eleven, stirred a bit but did not open his eyes. If he had opened them, he would have seen more than a hundred men, a few lying on the ground wrapped in their blankets, but most of them already up and moving about.

It was the last week of September in the year 1758. The sun had not risen, but dawn was beginning to break over Lake Ontario. It was especially welcome to this group on the shore of a little bay at the western end of the lake. For fourteen days they had been on their way from Montreal, in large canoes laden with provisions for Fort Niagara.

⋙ 1 →

Most of the men were voyageurs, accustomed to paddling their canoes in all sorts of weather; but Philippe de Croix, the one boy in the company, had been used to living in a house and having a bed to sleep in. He had suffered no great hardship, however, for they had all been kind to him; and on rainy nights he had slept under one of the canoes turned upside down.

The glow of pink and gold in the east brought a note of joy to Pierre's voice, as again he called, "Wake up, Philippe! This is no morning to delay the fleet. If we get early start, we'll be at Fort Niagara by night."

At the first call, Philippe had thought he was back in the village in France, where he had been born and had lived until a few months before. At the magic words, "Fort Niagara," he recalled that he was not in France but in America. He was only one day's journey from the father he loved, who had been sent to America to fight against the English in what we call "The French and Indian War" or "The Seven Years' War."

Philippe had expected to find his father at Montreal, but when he landed at the end of his long voyage, he was met at the dock by a man dressed in fringed buckskin, with a cap of red wool on his head.

"I am Pierre," the voyageur had said with a

smile. "Captain de Croix, he was ordered to Fort Niagara a week ago. He very sorry not to be here to welcome you. He ask me to take you up there on my next trip."

So Philippe had been in a canoe with Pierre all these days and had grown fond of him. When the boy was wide awake, he jumped to his feet, rolled up the blanket in which he had been sleeping, and went down to the lake, where the little waves were gently coming in on the narrow pebbly beach. He drank the cool water. He washed his face and hands. He smoothed his hair.

Forty canoes were drawn up on the narrow shore. They had been filled with barrels of pork, sacks of flour, bags of salt, bales of blankets, boxes of trinkets, cases of guns, kegs of rum and of molasses.

When the men had landed the night before, they had taken out the heavier things, lest when the canoes were drawn up on the beach, they should break with the weight of the load. With the smaller bales and bundles still inside, they had lifted the canoes to a safe place out of the water. Now they were beginning to reload them, in order to start as soon as possible after breakfast.

"Antoine, fetch that keg over here and put it

⋙ 3 →

in my canoe," shouted Pierre to a man who was taking a certain keg to another canoe.

"What difference does it make, which canoe it goes into?" grumbled Antoine. "Don't we all go to the same place?"

"Never mind where we are going. That keg is in my care. No one else shall take it," ordered Pierre.

It was not the first time Antoine had tried to get hold of that particular keg—the one with the red stripe around it. Every one had been wondering what it contained, that Pierre should value it so highly and not allow it in any canoe but his own.

No one dared disobey Pierre, however; so, with some grumbling, the keg was brought over to his canoe and stowed safely away.

Philippe, too, wondered what could be in it. It must be something very precious, for Pierre to care so much. Possibly the voyageur noticed the questioning look in the boy's eyes, for he remarked:

"That keg has something I promised to take safe to Detroit. Why need they know what's in it?"

The cook was already frying some fish that had been caught the night before. How good they smelled! How good they would taste!

Finally every one was up and they all ate

eagerly of the fish and bread. It made men hungry to be in the open air day and night.

Before long the canoes had been pushed off into the water, had been reloaded and were on their way eastward, keeping close together, skirting the southwestern shore of Lake Ontario. In each one were four or six men, French Canadians who spent their lives going up and down the lakes and rivers of America, paddling canoes.

Philippe was puzzled by their going toward the rising sun.

"Why do we go east today?" he asked.

"If we had come along the south shore of the lake," Pierre replied, "we would have reached Niagara by going west all the way, but the English, they might have captured us. They have a fort on that shore—Fort Oswego."

"I see," said Philippe. "We had to come by the north shore to the western end of the lake, and now we are going back east along this south shore to reach Niagara."

"That is it," said Pierre. "We have only about forty miles to go today."

The glow of pink and gold that morning made a sparkling path of color stretching from the canoes toward the rising sun. Hour after hour they went on, Pierre's canoe in the lead, following the forest-covered shore.

When they had been going about an hour, Philippe asked:

"Why do we not see any houses and farms or cities and villages along the shore? Is there nothing but forest in New France?"

"Quebec and Three Rivers and Montreal, you have seen them," said Pierre. "They are the cities of New France. We passed by some villages and farms along the St. Lawrence. Don't you remember? But everywhere else it is nothing but forest, with forts here and there."

"But why do not the French settle here in villages and have farms as we do in France?"

"It is not the same here, in our part of America. The great forests must be cut down before one can have a village or a farm. The French do not like to live in a wilderness. So those whom you will find here are mostly trappers and traders who travel the forest and soldiers who live in the forts."

"But you are not a trapper or a trader or a soldier, are you?"

"I? I am a voyageur. I paddle a canoe, carrying things from one place to another. I always go up and down the lakes and rivers. It is the grand life."

Pierre never stopped the steady stroke of his paddle, as he replied to these questions. After a few moments Philippe asked, "Why do our French people come here?"

"For the fur trade. All through the winter, the trappers are busy catching animals that have good furs—the beaver, the fox, the marten, the otter. In the spring they bring them down to the trading posts. There is much money in furs."

"But why did my father have to be sent away out here?"

"Your father is a soldier. The soldiers come for the glory of France and in the service of the King, our great King Louis. They defend New France against the English. The Lilies of France, long shall they wave over Niagara!"

In the canoe there were two soldiers, going to join the garrison at Fort Niagara. One of these, Sergeant La Barre, now spoke up: "When officers like your father are at Fort Niagara, the English can never make it surrender."

Philippe watched the sparkling ripples for a long time; then he asked: "What are the French and the English fighting about?"

"You can think of many questions," said Pierre. "I'll let Sergeant La Barre answer that one."

"The English, who live in the eastern part of America, want to settle in our territory. They want to get our fur trade away from us. Is it not so, Pierre?" asked the Sergeant.

"That is it," agreed Pierre. "They are always stealing into our part of America and trying to settle there. They have no right to do that."

"Fort Niagara is one of the main forts in New France," said the Sergeant. "It is most important that we French should keep it."

"We voyageurs," said Pierre, "we do our best to take food up to Niagara before the cold weather sets in, so that the soldiers will not go hungry this winter. They defend the Fort against the English. We must take food to them. We must take blankets and guns and powder and everything else they need."

The talking ceased and the boatmen kept their paddles going in a rhythmic swing, sometimes joining in a jolly song as they paddled along.

Late in the afternoon a storm came up. The thunder rolled. The wind blew hard from the northwest. Whitecaps appeared on the lake. Rain began to fall and drenched them.

"Shall we try to make a landing?" asked one of the men.

"We had better head for the mouth of the river. See, there it is," replied Pierre.

The men bent to their paddles, as they turned toward the south to enter the Niagara.

It took all the skill of the voyageurs to keep

the canoes right side up, but fortunately the wind from the northwest helped them along.

Once Pierre spoke to Philippe, "There is Fort Niagara ahead."

Philippe looked at the gray walls of the Fort, standing where the Niagara River flows into the lake. His heart beat fast as he realized that he would soon be with his father, whom he had not seen for two years.

# CHAPTER II

## ARRIVAL AT FORT NIAGARA

HE rain ceased as they entered the mouth of the mighty river. Philippe could now see the Fort more plainly on his left. Great waves came sweeping into the river from the northwest.

Usually the canoes and bateaux landed at a little dock near the mouth of the river. The cargoes were unloaded there and carried up the slope to a small gate on the western side of the Fort. It was called the "river gate," or the "Niagara gate." A little farther up the river, there was a cove and a sandy beach, where the boats could land in case of storm. Then the cargoes were carried up to the large gate, called "The Gate of the Five Nations."

As the canoes came into the river, one of the men shouted, "Shall we try to land at the dock?"

"No, we never could do it," replied Pierre. "See the waves dashing over it. We'll go on up to the cove."

A quarter of a mile farther on, they rounded

a bend into the little cove, where the water was calmer. The boatmen slowed up their canoes and finally stopped paddling, letting them glide up to the little sandy beach.

Philippe wondered whether his father would be down at the beach. He scanned the faces of the men on shore, who had come hurrying up to the cove when they saw the fleet of canoes pass the dock.

Most of those on shore were Indians of the Seneca tribe, whose business it was to help unload the canoes. Soon there was great activity on the river bank, Indians and Canadians carrying bundles and bales up the slope toward the gate.

Among the crowd, Philippe kept looking for the one face he was eager to see.

"Your father, he may be busy with duties he cannot leave," said Pierre kindly.

"If he were well, he would surely be here to meet me," said Philippe.

"Perhaps he hasn't heard that the fleet is in. Fort Niagara, it is a big place, with many buildings. He'll be glad to see you, of that you may be sure."

At that moment an Indian boy of about Philippe's age came running down to the dock. He reached out his hands for a bundle.

"Me carry," he said.

Pierre handed him a small one and then said to Philippe, "Here is a comrade for you. This

is Red Bird, a boy of the Iroquois. You will have good times together."

Red Bird looked in amazement at Philippe's fine clothes. Philippe looked with equal surprise at the Indian boy's bare feet and legs.

Philippe took the little chest he had brought all the way from France and started up the slope behind Pierre, who carried a barrel of flour on his shoulder. Red Bird followed, with his bundle swung over his shoulder.

There was now a long line of men walking up the slope toward the gate, each carrying a sack, a barrel or a bundle.

As they were coming through the gate into the grounds of the Fort, Philippe was startled by the sound

of a cannon and showed it by a sudden little jump. Red Bird looked at him with astonishment.

Pierre smiled and said, "It won't be long, my Philippe, till you are used to life in a fort. You'll not jump at the sound of a sunset gun when you have been here a week."

Red Bird glanced out of the corner of his eye at this strange lad, with clothes so different from those of the captive children sometimes brought to the Fort.

"Where does he come from? Why did he come?" thought the Indian lad.

"Come to the storehouse. I must report to the storekeeper," said Pierre to Philippe. "When I am through, then we hunt up your father."

Philippe stood at the open door of the store-house, while Pierre and the storekeeper began to check up the articles.

"Is everything to be left here?" asked the storekeeper.

"No; only half. The rest is for Detroit. We start in a few days."

Philippe looked at the many buildings inside the ramparts of the Fort. The largest was a stone building that looked like a large dwelling house, at the far side of the grounds. It was called "the Castle." There were two or three long low buildings used for storehouses. There was a bake-house and a powder house. There were cabins for the gunsmiths and barracks for the soldiers.

"I wonder which building my father is in," thought Philippe.

He had not long to wonder. Word had gone forth that a fleet of canoes had arrived from Montreal. Through the gathering twilight there soon came striding a tall officer, in a brilliant uniform. As he saw the boy, he quickened his pace and came on the run.

"Oh, Philippe! My Philippe!" he exclaimed.

"Father!" exclaimed the boy; and they were in each other's arms.

"Thank God, you got here safe," said Captain de Croix. "Where is Pierre, that I may thank him for bringing you to me?"

"He is in the storehouse, counting the bundles and bales. He was very kind to me all the way up from Montreal."

"He would be," said the Captain. "Pierre has the best heart in the world. We'll see him and thank him together."

"This Niagara is far off. We were a long time on the way."

"Yes; it is far off and it is a lonely place, but now I shall be lonely no more."

When Pierre came out of the storehouse, Captain de Croix said, *"Merci, mon Pierre! I shall* never forget this kindness you have done in bringing my Philippe here."

"It was nothing," answered Pierre. "The lad was no trouble. I think he'll be a voyageur when he is older. I'll take him on a long trip sometime."

"In case we stay in America," said the Captain; "but this war will be over before long. Then I shall be sent back to France and Philippe will go with me."

As it was getting dark, he turned to Philippe and said:

"Come, we will go to the Castle and I will show you our room. We'll get some supper, too. You must be hungry."

"I do not care whether I have any supper," said Philippe. "Now that I am with you, nothing else matters. Oh, Father, how lonely I was after you went away!"

As they were walking across the parade ground, Philippe saw many soldiers. When they passed the gunsmith's cabin, he saw the glare of the forge shining through the open door. The heavy wooden door of the Castle stood open. They passed through the vestibule, a large entrance room; then under a broad stone arch to a corridor and on to a room where several officers were sitting around a table.

"He has come!" said Captain de Croix joyfully. "My son has come!"

"Good!" said the Commandant, rising.

"He is most welcome," said Father Joseph, the kindly, middle-aged chaplain.

One after another, the officers welcomed Philippe and expressed joy at his safe arrival. The Captain sent a servant to the great kitchen for food, which Philippe ate hungrily.

When he had finished his supper, though he was interested in this strange new place, his eyes became heavy and he could scarcely keep them open. He had not had a wink of sleep since the moment before dawn, when Pierre had come to him on the shore of Lake Ontario and had said, "Wake up, Philippe! Wake up!"

"Don't keep the lad awake longer," said Captain Du Charme. "Another evening he must tell us about our France."

"Come with me upstairs to our room," said Captain de Croix.

They went to a small winding stairway near the front door. When they reached the second floor, they entered one of the rooms reserved for the officers.

In one corner of the room there was a bed built against the wall. On it there was a straw mattress and blankets. It even had sheets, which the beds of the common soldiers did not have.

By the time they reached the room, Philippe's drowsiness was gone. He was eager to answer his father's questions about people and things in France. He was eager to tell about his voyage.

For half an hour they talked; then Philippe opened his small chest and began to take out some of the things.

"See, Father, what I brought all the way," said he.

He took out a handsome coat, such as the gentlemen of that day wore on grand occasions. It was made of pale green brocaded satin and trimmed with much gold thread arranged in a beautiful design that made it look like lace. When Philippe had first seen it, he had called it "the gold-laced coat," and always afterward the family had so spoken of it.

"My gold-laced coat!" exclaimed Captain de Croix. "Well, it seems good to see that again. What fine days those were when I wore it at Court and attended the King!"

"I remember, Father. You looked so grand. I have kept it in my room all this time and have looked at it the last thing every night. You did not seem so far away when I looked at that."

"And were you very lonely?" asked Captain de Croix.

"Oh, yes, indeed. I didn't like it at cousin Raoul's house, he was so stern and cross. He kept me locked in a closet all one day, because I forgot to bow low to him the first thing in the morning."

"The rascal! If I had known that, I would have sent for you sooner. America has not all the advantages that France has, but you and I

will at least not be lonely. We'll have many a good time together. Let me put the coat on."

He put on the coat, so richly emblazoned, and stood there erect.

Philippe clapped his hands. "You are a very grand gentleman," he said.

"It was a load for you to bring that all the

way from France. How did you manage to get everything in that little chest?"

"I did not have many things of my own to bring; and I packed them in close, for I would not leave that coat behind. It is my most precious treasure."

Captain de Croix smiled. "It is wonderful to have you here, my son! You had better go to bed now. You may hang the coat on that peg at the foot of the bed."

So the boy from France went to sleep that first night in Fort Niagara, with the gleaming coat the last thing his eyes fell on, in the light of the candle flame.

# CHAPTER III

## THE DOLL FROM PARIS

HILIPPE and his father ate their breakfast the next morning at the long table in the huge kitchen of the Castle. The rooms in the first story had stone floors and thick walls of stone. They were all dark, with only tiny windows; but Philippe thought this kitchen was an interesting and homelike place, with its great fireplace, the strings of corn and the hams hanging from the beams overhead, the huge wooden mixing trough, and the great kettles hanging over the fire.

"I am very busy with my duties through the day," said Captain de Croix, "so you may go off by yourself and look around. Go where you please inside the Fort, but do not go outside today."

"Are there English soldiers near?" asked Philippe. "Is that why I may not go outside?"

"No; there are probably no English soldiers nearer than Fort Oswego; and that is over a hundred miles east of here. But there might be Indians who are on the side of the English. They would be only too glad to capture the son of a French officer."

"I'll stay inside," said Philippe.

He had heard stories of boys and girls taken captive by the Indians.

"Red Bird will be in the Fort after a while," said the Captain. "He will show you around and he may want you to go outside. He is safe from capture himself and he might not think about your danger."

"Never fear. I am not sure that I like Red Bird."

"Red Bird is a brave lad and a useful one. He does many errands for us. He even goes into dangerous places to do things for us. He lights the fires in the big ovens in the bake-house. You will like him when you are acquainted."

"How does he happen to live here?"

"His parents are dead. His father was one of the Indians who unload the canoes. Red Bird goes in and out of the Fort as he pleases."

"I'll go around by myself."

"You will find many interesting things here in the Fort, and many interesting people, too. From time to time there will be Indians from many tribes, Indians from the Ohio country, Indians from the far west, Indians from the

Iroquois. You will see canoe-men or voyageurs, you will see traders and trappers. You will see soldiers from France and from Canada. Fort Niagara is a busy place, even if it is off in the wilderness."

Captain de Croix went to his duties and Philippe stepped outside the Castle, or "Mess-house," as it was sometimes called. He looked around at the many buildings inside the walls. To his right, near one corner of the Castle, was the bake-house his father had mentioned, a small stone building. To his left, overlooking the lake, were four Lombardy poplars standing in a row. Across the parade ground were several long low buildings, barracks for the soldiers. In another direction was the storehouse where they had been the night before. There were many other buildings, all built of logs except the powder magazine, which was of stone.

Not far from the poplars was a chapel which the soldiers called "the big chapel," to distinguish it from the one inside the Castle.

"Where is Pierre?" the boy was wondering, when the voyageur himself came along.

"Good morning, Philippe," he said. "How do you like Fort Niagara?"

"I like it very much," replied Philippe. "It is a bigger place than I supposed it would be."

"I come over here to ask a favor," Pierre went on.

"What is it? I'd like to do something for you."

"That oak keg, do you remember it?"

"Oh, yes; the one with the red stripe, in which there is something very precious."

"I wish to get it safe to Detroit, when I go on in a few days. Some of the canoe-men are eager to get that keg away from me. Especially is Antoine bent on getting it."

"Why does Antoine want to do that?"

"He seems to hold a grudge against me. I think it is because I scolded him, when he was careless with supplies we were loading at Montreal. I can look out for it myself when we are on the way. No one will meddle with Pierre's things then; but while I am at the Fort, going here and there, I cannot keep track of it. If only I could put it in a safe place in the Castle!"

"Put it in our room," Philippe offered.

"Thank you. That is just what I'd like to do," replied Pierre.

He saluted and went to fetch the keg. When Philippe had led the way to their room and the keg was safely stowed in a corner, Pierre said, "Can you keep a secret, Philippe? If you can, I'll tell you what is in the keg."

"I promise," Philippe said promptly.

"Well, at Detroit there is a little girl named Marie, the daughter of one of the officers. Her father ordered for her a beautiful doll from Paris. It was arranged that I bring it from Montreal when it arrived from France. Some one must take it who would be very careful. Was it not a big thing, Philippe, to be chosen for such a task?"

Philippe looked with great admiration at this kind man, who thought it a privilege to be given a troublesome task.

"When it came, packed in a wooden case, I knew that if it should fall into the water along the route, it would be ruined," said Pierre. "So, what did I do, after thinking for a whole day, but decide to put the case inside a stout keg that would be water tight? I found the best oak keg in Montreal. I put around it extra hoops to make it strong. Then I placed in it the case containing the doll and packed blankets around. The little Marie, she is the sunshine of the Fort all the long winter. I'll get the doll to her safe and dry."

"But what if Antoine does get it?" asked Philippe.

"Just let him try," said Pierre. "I have no fear, if only I can keep it away from him here at the Fort."

"It is safe now. The guard will not let any-one in."

When they came out of the Castle they saw the flag waving in the breeze. They stood and saluted it, the banner of France, golden fleurs-de-lis on a field of white. Philippe could never look at it without a thrill of pride in his country.

"I must go down to the landing now," said Pierre.

After he had gone a few steps, he came back and said, "You may tell Red Bird what is in the keg, if you wish, but no one else."

Glancing toward the bake-house, Philippe saw the baker standing in the door, beckoning him to come over.

"Well, well!" said the baker. "Who are you? When did you come? It is good to see some-body just from France. What is your name, son?"

"I am Philippe, the son of Captain de Croix. I arrived last night from Montreal with the fleet."

"But you came farther than from Montreal," said the baker.

"Oh, yes, I have lately come from France. When I reached Montreal my father had been ordered here. So Pierre brought me up in his canoe."

"That Pierre!" said the baker. "A fine fellow, but he never stays long in one place."

"He was very kind to me," said Philippe.

"Have you seen that Indian boy this morning?" suddenly asked the baker. "He lights the fire for me. Why hasn't he come?"

"Maybe I could light it," offered Philippe. "How do you do it?"

"No, you could not," said the baker. "It takes some one who knows just how to lay the wood and apply the torch. One has to crawl into the oven and light it at the farther end."

"I could try," said Philippe.

As he turned toward the oven, he noticed the huge wooden mixing trough, in which the dough had been mixed.

"What a big batch of dough!" he exclaimed.

"It requires a great deal of bread to feed so many soldiers," said the baker. "Besides the soldiers, there are always Indians coming to be fed; there are the canoe-men and traders constantly coming this way."

Philippe looked inside one of the two huge ovens. It was ten or twelve feet long from front to back, with a flat floor and a curved roof. A log about six inches in diameter had already been shoved into it.

"You are to place the sticks of wood crisscross over the log, the whole length of it," said

the baker. "Then I'll give you the torch to
light the fire."

Philippe started to do it, but just then Red
Bird appeared in the doorway.

"White boy better not," said Red Bird.
"Might get burned."

He crawled into the oven and laid the sticks
of wood carefully over the log; then he was
handed a blazing torch. He lighted the kindling at the back of the oven and then scrambled
out backward. The baker drew out the log,
thus leaving a draft for the fire. Soon the
crackling of the flames could be heard.

"Here," said the baker, as he handed the Indian boy a piece of bread for his breakfast.

"That is Red Bird's pay for lighting our fire,"
he said to Philippe.

"Isn't it dangerous to crawl into the oven?"
asked Philippe.

"There is no danger," said the baker. "A
larger person couldn't do it, but Red Bird is
safe, as he is small. Now you two boys run off
and have a good time together."

It was the same thing the voyageur had said.
Philippe kept thinking how different Red Bird
was from the boys he knew back in France. He
drew back a bit.

"Red Bird, take Philippe around and show

him the things in the Fort," said the baker. "He has come here to live."

Red Bird said something, but in a language Philippe had never heard. The baker interpreted: "Red Bird says he will show you the Fort. He knows some French, for he hears it spoken a great deal; but he is a bit timid about using it till he knows you better. You need not be afraid to go with him. He is proud to be with the son of Captain de Croix."

The two boys went out the door together.

# CHAPTER IV

## FUR TRADING

ATE in the afternoon of Philippe's first day at Fort Niagara, he was aware of a sound, a dull roar, which came frequently to his ears.

"What is that sound?" he asked. "It seems to come from the forest, off in that direction."

He pointed toward the south, up the river.

"The Falls," answered Red Bird.

"The Falls?" questioned Philippe.

Red Bird tried to tell, but with the many Indian words he used, Philippe could make little of it.

They were near the gunsmith's cabin, and went in to see him work. The flare of the forge made a pleasant sight this chilly day, as he was repairing a musket.

"That roar?" he said, in answer to Philippe's question. "That is Niagara Falls. You have heard of that great cataract, haven't you?"

"Yes; is it near by?" asked Philippe. "I'd like to see it."

"Not very near. About six leagues up the river toward the south. The water goes pouring over the brink with a tremendous roar. We do not hear it except on a damp day or just before a storm or when the wind is in the right direction. Probably we are going to have a storm."

Philippe stepped to the door and looked up to the sky, which was already becoming overcast with clouds.

"Sometime you must go up the river and see the Falls," said the gunsmith. "It is a wonderful sight."

As the two boys left the cabin, they saw a number of Indians coming through the small gate, carrying packs.

"Who are they? What have they in those packs?" asked Philippe.

"Furs," said Red Bird.

A soldier standing near spoke up: "They are Indians from the far west, come with pelts. They are from the Illinois country or beyond."

"How far is that?" asked Philippe.

"More than five hundred miles."

"Five hundred miles!" exclaimed Philippe. "What a big country this must be!"

The soldier laughed. "Big! Why, lad, one

could travel for months straight west and never come to the end of it."

There were three Indians in the group, part of a band that had come down the lakes in thirty canoes. The rest were staying outside the Fort while these did their trading, as only a small number were admitted at one time.

Philippe followed them to the trading room in the Castle.

One of the Indians, opening his bale of furs, took from it a beaver skin and held it up for the storekeeper to see; then he laid it on the counter of rough planks.

"Beads," he said.

The storekeeper placed on the rough counter a pouch of deerskin containing beads of bright colors. After much dickering as to how many beads should be given for the pelt, the storekeeper handed him the beads and took the beaver skin.

The Indian took another pelt from his pile.

"Blanket," he said.

The storekeeper took down a cheap blanket from a shelf.

"No; good blanket," said the Indian.

"It will take three pelts," said the storekeeper.

The Indian shook his head.

"These skins are not so good as those caught

in the winter," said the storekeeper. "You will have to give three."

The Indian reluctantly took two more beaver skins from the bale. By the time he had traded all his pelts, there was in his pile, besides the beads and the blanket, some knives, some little

mirrors, some bright ribbons, a kettle and some long gay feathers, dyed green, red and yellow.

The next Indian stepped up to the counter.

"Gun," he said.

The storekeeper brought out a long musket, more than five feet long. He stood it up against the counter.

The Indian began to pile up beaver skins, one

on top of another, till they reached about a foot below the top of the musket.

"Enough," he said. "Many as last time."

"But this is a better gun. See, it is longer," said the storekeeper.

The Indian looked puzzled. If they were to make the pile of pelts high enough to reach the top of such a long gun, it would take very many skins of the beaver or the fox.

Some soldiers came in to watch the trading. After a little hesitation, the Indian placed two more skins on the pile. Still they did not reach the top of the gun.

"Enough," he protested.

The soldiers looked at each other and winked. They knew the guns had been made longer than those of last year, so that the Indians would have to give more furs in trade.

"No, not enough," declared the storekeeper. "Three more."

Slowly the Indian placed the additional furs on the pile, which now reached the top of the musket. He took the gun, examined it and held it out.

"Long gun!" he said.

When they had finished their trading and had gone out of the Fort, another group of three came to the trading room. The rest of the band waited until the next day.

Philippe and Red Bird watched the trading go on. Not all the Indians chose beads and blankets and guns. Some chose knives or salt or axes. Some chose bright ribbons for the Indian girls or bright cloth from which the Indian women could make clothes. Some chose a kettle or a sack of flour.

When they were through, the bales of furs filled a large space in the storehouse. They would be sent down to Montreal in canoes, and then in a ship over to Paris, to make warm coats and robes for the people of France.

That night Philippe was awakened by the sound of rain which came pelting on his window.

The words of the gunsmith came to his mind.

"The prophecy was true," he thought. "The Falls *did* foretell a storm."

## CHAPTER V

### RED BIRD LIGHTS THE OVEN

HROUGH a dense fog, Philippe went to the bake-house the next morning, when it was time to light the fire. The huge batch of bread was already rising in the great wooden trough. The oven door stood open and Red Bird was on hand.

How many times Red Bird had lighted the fire for the baker! Perhaps it was a hundred times, perhaps three hundred. He crawled into the oven through the door at the front. He began to place the sticks of wood over the log, crisscross, as usual. He was still working at it when an Indian came from the landing place with a message.

"What is it, Flying Wind?" asked the baker, as the Indian stood in the doorway.

"Henri, he starting for Montreal. He want to see you before he go."

The baker took up a pine torch and gave it to Philippe, saying, "Will you hand this to Red Bird when he is ready for it?"

Philippe took the torch and replied, "Yes, I'll give it to him."

"I won't be gone long," said the baker, as he left with the Indian.

Philippe stood waiting, as Red Bird worked in the oven. When he called for the torch, Philippe reached into the oven and handed it to him.

Red Bird held it against the kindling until some of the pieces caught fire. Then he started to scramble out backward. Whether he was a bit excited this morning, when Philippe was watching, or whether the fire started to burn faster than usual, no one ever knew; but, quickly raising his head too high, he bumped it on the roof of the oven and fell flat on the oven floor, stunned.

Philippe, hearing the crackling of the flames, looked in. Red Bird was lying very still, his feet just inside the door. At the farther end, the wood was burning and sending forth smoke. The heavy fog seemed to keep the smoke in, instead of letting it rise through the chimney.

"Red Bird! Red Bird!" Philippe called.

There was no answer. There was no movement of Red Bird's feet, wriggling to creep backward.

"Red Bird! Hurry!" shouted Philippe.

Still there was no answer.

"Oh! What has happened to him?" cried Philippe, not knowing what to do.

He looked anxiously toward the door, but there was no baker in sight. Frantically, he took hold of Red Bird's feet and started to pull him out.

Carefully he pulled till he had the Indian boy out of the oven and let him down gently to the stone floor. There seemed to be no life in the lad.

Placing his own jacket under Red Bird's head, Philippe ran out of the bake-house, across the parade ground toward the quarters of the doctor in the hospital. He almost ran into Sergeant La Barre.

"What is your hurry?" asked the Sergeant.

"Red Bird. In the bake-house," answered Philippe, without stopping to explain.

The Sergeant ran over there. He threw some water in Red Bird's face.

Philippe found the doctor and exclaimed, "Red Bird! Come quick! Bake-house!"

Then he turned and ran back. The doctor followed him on the run. When he had examined Red Bird, he said, "The lad is nearly suffocated with smoke. Here is a bad burn on his hand, too."

Philippe watched the doctor working on the Indian boy. He found that he cared very much whether Red Bird could be revived, and he rejoiced when there were signs of life.

"You came just in time," said the doctor. "In a few minutes more, he would have been beyond my skill."

"Will he get well?" asked Philippe.

"I think so."

After a bit, Red Bird opened his eyes and looked around.

"You nearly smothered with the smoke in the oven," said the doctor.

"Who take me out?" he asked.

"It was Philippe," said the doctor. "If he had not pulled you out of the oven and run for me, you might have died."

Sergeant La Barre and the doctor carried him over to the hospital, where the doctor dressed his hand. Philippe went over to see him toward night.

"I hope you are better," he said.

Red Bird looked at him and said; "Me all right. Never forget. Your friend, forever."

"And I'll be your friend, too," said Philippe.

# CHAPTER VI

 **T**HAT evening Philippe sat with his father and the other officers in one of the rooms of the Castle, around a blazing fire. Pierre was with them. They liked to have him there, for he had news to tell and could sing for them and play on his fiddle.

"Give us a song, Pierre," said Father Joseph. Pierre took up the fiddle and began—

> *A la claire fontaine*
> *M'en allant promener,*
> *J'ai trouvé l'eau si belle*
> *Que je m'y suis baigné.*
> *Il y a longtemps que je t'aime,*
> *Jamais je ne t'oublierai.*

There was a round of applause as he finished. Again and again he sang for them the songs of New France, the songs the voyageurs sang as they dipped their paddles. Then the officers fell to talking.

"You have just come from Montreal, Pierre;

tell us, what are the officials there doing to get supplies to us for the winter? Did you hear much about it?" asked Captain de Croix.

"Oh, yes," replied Pierre eagerly. "They are getting all the voyageurs around that country to paddle bateaux and canoes up here with supplies. Some say there are a thousand."

"The English were clever to destroy Fort Frontenac just when it was full of supplies for our French forts," remarked Lieutenant Le Maire.

"Yes, but it was unlucky for us when they sank all our ships," said Captain Du Charme.

"Not all were sunk," said Pierre; "only seven, and the other two were carried off to Fort Oswego."

"They're of no use to us," said the Lieutenant, "whether they are at the bottom of Lake Ontario or in the hands of the enemy."

"We'll try to bring plenty," Pierre assured them.

Fort Frontenac had stood on the north shore of Lake Ontario, at its outlet into the St. Lawrence River, where the Canadian city of Kingston now stands. Here had been stored the goods for Niagara and the forts beyond, Presque Isle, Le Boeuf, Venango, Duquesne, Detroit and others. In previous years French sailing ships had brought from Frontenac food for the forts and goods for the Indian trade, enough each fall to last all winter.

But in August of this year, 1758, the English General Bradstreet had captured Fort Frontenac and all the supplies, and had sunk or captured all the French ships. Dismay filled the hearts of the French at Niagara, when they heard of it. What would they do for food this winter? What would they do for goods to trade with the Indians?

It was Pierre and other voyageurs who were solving the problem, paddling canoes and bateaux with supplies from Montreal to these forts.

"Are you going back now for more supplies, Pierre?" asked Lieutenant Marchand.

"No; not yet. I go on to Detroit with a fleet first. I start tomorrow. Then I come back and go down the lake for another load."

"Is there a fleet starting west tomorrow?" asked Captain de Croix.

"Yes," replied Pierre. "We go up the Portage early in the morning."

"Then you will want your keg," said Philippe.

"Yes, I come and get it as soon as you are up."

"What is a portage?" suddenly asked Philippe. "How do you go up one?"

Pierre replied: "A portage is a carrying-place. Many times when we are going along a river, we come to rapids, where the canoes cannot go. We have to take them out of the water and carry them around the rapids. Did you ever see rapids, Philippe?"

"Only those in the St. Lawrence River, when we came up in the canoe."

"Oh, yes; but there it was possible to take the canoes through. Those in the Niagara are much more dangerous."

When Pierre was excited, he often talked brokenly. Now he went on: "In rapids the water go over rocks; it jump up; it rush swiftly; it make lovely white spray. Rapids very beautiful to look at, but most terrible for boats. In this Niagara River, the rapids are the worst of all. The water, it boil; it plunge; it rush madly. And then there are the great Falls. Can a boat go up the face of a cataract?"

"No," said Philippe. "I have never seen a cataract, but I have seen pictures of them. A canoe never could do it."

Pierre laughed at the idea. "The boat would have to go straight up, nearly two hundred feet. Could she do it? That is why there is a portage here, the most difficult in America."

Captain de Croix spoke: "Some day, Philippe, I would like you to go up the Portage and see this great cataract. It is most marvelous. You would go in a canoe seven miles up the river. At that point, on the east side, a high ridge starts from the river and goes east nearly a hundred miles. It is so high that it has always been called the 'Mountain.' The water goes faster beyond that, so the canoes have to be taken out of the river and carried up that high mountain ridge. All the cargo has to be taken out and carried up. Then, at the top, there are still eight miles to the end of the Portage, above the Falls. There the canoes are put into the river again. It is all very interesting. Perhaps I can get away to go up there with you, after a while."

Philippe's eyes sparkled. Wouldn't he like to go up that Portage and see the great Falls?

Pierre spoke up, "Why not let him go with me tomorrow? We'll have many things to carry up the hill, and he can see how it is done. From the end of the Portage at Fort Little Niagara, it is only a short walk, less than a league down to the Falls."

"You will be going on west," said the Captain. "I don't think best for him to come back alone or with strangers. There are always Indians friendly to the English, prowling around the Portage."

"I know a man who is coming back the next day," said Pierre. "A friend of mine who can be trusted is on his way to Montreal. I manage it."

"May I go, Father?" asked Philippe eagerly.

Captain de Croix did not reply at once, but said, "I wonder if Red Bird could go along. Yes, if Red Bird can go, Philippe may go, too."

"I'll find Red Bird and tell him," said Pierre. "The lads must be ready at sunrise."

Pierre went out of the Castle. The group broke up, Philippe and his father going to their room.

"What are these other forts that must have supplies?" asked Philippe. "Where are they?"

On the wall there hung a map of New France, sketched on deerskin.

"I will show you on this map," said his father.

He gave Philippe a stick with which to point to the places.

"After Fort Niagara, here at the mouth of the Niagara River, the first one is at the other end of the Portage. It is called 'Fort Little Niagara.' It is on the bank of the river, about a mile and a half above the great Falls. The next one is called Presque Isle and is on the south shore of Lake Erie."

As Philippe pointed to it, he said, "That seems a long way from here."

"Yes; it is over a hundred miles. The next one is south of that one, Fort Le Boeuf. Still farther south is Fort Venango and then Fort

Duquesne. They are all important. There is a fort called Vincennes, away out west."

"I see it," exclaimed Philippe. "That is very far off in the wilderness."

"Yes," said his father. "Then, if we should go along the north shore of Lake Erie, after leaving Little Niagara, the first fort is at Detroit. If we go on farther west, there are still others. All these forts are dependent on Niagara, where we are. Every canoe-load of supplies has to go past Fort Niagara to reach those forts. Every load of furs from those forts and the country around them, has to come down the Portage and past Niagara. This is a very important place for France. The Portage, up which you are going tomorrow, is a most important road. Do you see that?"

Philippe studied the map a few moments longer. "Yes, I see it," he said. "I am glad you told me before we start."

Captain de Croix then sat down at his desk to write a letter, and Philippe got ready for bed.

In a few minutes his father showed him the letter and said, "Philippe, I wish you to carry this to the Commandant at Fort Little Niagara, Sieur de Chabert, who is a friend of mine. You must give it to him and to no one else."

"I'll be sure to give it to him," Philippe replied. "How shall I find him?"

"If he is at the Fort now, there will be no difficulty, but he is away a great deal on expeditions among the Indians. If he is away, bring the letter back to me."

"Yes, Father. If I cannot give it to Sieur de Chabert, I am to bring it back."

"Quite right. If he is there, he may wish you to bring an answer back. Do not give it to anyone but me."

"Yes, Father, I will be sure," said Philippe, feeling very important to be trusted with his father's affairs.

# CHAPTER VII

HE Niagara is a short river. Compared with the Mississippi, the Amazon or the Nile, it is insignificant. It is only thirty-seven miles long from its source, at the outlet of Lake Erie, to its mouth, where it flows into Lake Ontario; but in that short distance there are more wonderful and interesting sights than on almost any other river in the world.

In its course it flows in rushing rapids over a rocky bed, falls with a tremendous roar over the brink of a high precipice, flows through a wide gorge two hundred feet deep, tosses and foams in the magnificent whirlpool rapids, and circles swiftly about in the huge whirlpool. Then, the last few miles of its course, it flows silently but swiftly between beautiful banks to the blue waters of a great lake.

Along its banks, much important history has been made. Three great nations have in turn ruled over it, France, Great Britain and the

United States. At the time of our story, it was in the hands of the French. Up and down its famous portage, there went bands of Indians and Frenchmen carrying furs on the way down and provisions, merchandise and military supplies on the way up. Indians from the Iroquois tribes in central New York, Indians from the Ohio country, Indians from the western tribes, came and went constantly. Traders, trappers, voyageurs and coureurs-de-bois (runners-of-the-woods) trod the Portage Road. Soldiers on their way to French forts to the west and south, all marched along it.

On the following morning, Philippe and Red Bird found themselves in one of the twenty canoes that started up the river. Each canoe was filled with provisions and merchandise for the western forts.

The two boys, wedged in by packages, sat on one of the bales of blankets in Pierre's canoe. Back of them was the keg he prized so much, its red stripe looking gay among the dull bundles and bales.

"Where are you taking all these things?" asked Philippe.

"To Detroit."

"Is that far?"

"Only about three hundred miles," answered Pierre.

"That is a long way to paddle a canoe."

Pierre laughed. "To me it is not far. I like to paddle a canoe. I like to be always going up and down the lakes and the rivers."

They were gliding along on the lower part of the river, between high banks brilliant with autumn leaves. The forests on each side were a glory of red and gold.

Not a house was to be seen on either hand, for at that time no white people lived along the banks of the Niagara, except in the forts.

A lovely sight it was, to see the fleet of canoes glide silently along on the blue water of the broad river.

When they had gone about seven miles, to the place where the village of Lewiston now stands, there loomed up on the east bank the great hill called the Mountain. The current was becoming stronger with every swing of the paddles and, not far beyond, were the terrible whirlpool and rapids.

Pierre, who was in the leading canoe, pulled in toward the landing. As they neared the shore, Philippe saw a number of Indians come down to help unload the canoes and carry the goods up the mountain. They were Indians from the Seneca tribe, who had a little village at the foot of the mountain.

"I don't see how they are ever going to get

Lake Ontario

Pt. Montreal

Fort Niagara

The Little Marsh

La Belle Famille

Site of Joncaire's trading-house

Lewiston Heights

Whirlpool

Portage Road

Fort Little Niagara (Cayuga)

Where the Griffon is supposed to have been built, 1679

R. Bois Blancs

The NIAGARA FRONTIER 1759

Niagara Falls

Grand Island

Scale of Miles

The Little Rapid

Lake Erie

those barrels and canoes up that big hill," said
Philippe.

"You'll see," said Red Bird, who had many
times gone up the Portage.

Such a commotion and hustling as there was
in unloading the canoes! Some of the Indians
took the smaller packs and started up the steep
rocky path, the packs on their backs. Then
Philippe saw them take the large things, the barrels and casks and huge bales. Finally they
lifted the canoes, each of which was carried upside down by two men over their heads.

"They can never do it," said Philippe.

"Never do what?" asked Pierre.

"Carry those canoes and those heavy things
all the way up that hill."

"Yes," said Pierre, "it is wonderful what
heavy loads these Indians can carry."

The two boys joined the line of men carrying
their heavy loads; but when they had gone a
little way, Philippe said, "I wish we could carry
something."

"We ask," said Red Bird.

They turned back and said to Pierre, "We
want to carry something up the hill."

"Here are some light bundles. Take these,"
he said, "but I warn you that you will find them
very heavy before you reach the top."

Philippe smiled. He would show them that

he could carry a fair load. He picked out a bundle of deerskin pouches containing beads and trinkets. They were heavy, those beads, heavier than he thought, but he wasn't going to back out after saying he would carry them.

Red Bird chose a lighter bundle. He knew how hard the climb would be. In places it would be so steep that one could scarcely keep a footing.

There were twenty canoes to be carried up. What a scene it was, there in the midst of the forest, with the broad beautiful river flowing by and the forest-covered mountain ahead!

The line of Indians and voyageurs, each carrying a pack on his back, went from the landing up the steep bank and turned south up the long portage hill.

Part way up the hill, there were some storehouses, where cargoes were sometimes left and then carried to the top later on; but this time everything was to be taken to the end of the Portage and started at once for Detroit.

The path was winding and narrow and, in places, very steep. The men, who were used to climbing the hill, were going steadily up without stopping, though at times they had to go nearly on all fours, because of the steepness of the grade. Red Bird, who was used to climbing in all sorts of places and who had taken the lighter pack, managed to keep going, in spite of the big rocks and big roots of trees and steep grades. But Philippe had never tried to climb anything so rough and steep before.

"I won't give up. I'll do it," he kept saying to himself.

He adjusted the bundle differently over his shoulder, took a few deep breaths, and started on, bound to keep his place in line.

When he had nearly reached the top, there came a place which was so very steep that Philippe felt himself slipping. He tried to grasp something but, the first thing he knew, he was tumbling downward. The pack slipped from his hands and his head hit a rock.

He knew no more till he opened his eyes with Red Bird and Pierre bending over him. They had carried him to a level spot and were bathing his head in cool water from a near-by tiny brook. There was a big bump on his head.

"I should have stayed behind you," said Pierre. "Those steep places are very hard to climb."

"I'll be all right," said Philippe. "I can stand up now."

He was a bit dizzy at first, but soon felt able to start on.

"I'll take your bundle," offered Pierre.

"No; I can do it," insisted Philippe. "If Red Bird can, I can."

He shouldered the bundle and again started up the slope. This time, following Pierre's advice to catch hold of a sapling, he succeeded in getting to the top of that particularly hard stretch of climbing.

Finally they all reached the top of the mountain, with the packs and bundles and barrels and canoes. From there the country lay in an almost level stretch for the eight miles to Fort Little Niagara, at the upper end of the Portage.

Sieur de Chabert, Commandant of that Fort, had a few horses and carts to carry loads on the Portage, but there were not enough for all the things that had come in the twenty canoes. So, after the carts were loaded, there were still many things left. The Indians swung these to their backs and started on to walk the eight miles.

Philippe and Red Bird had been glad to put their packs on one of the carts, and they now walked along with Pierre, who was carrying one end of his canoe. It was a rough dirt road, overgrown with grass in places, full of humps and hollows, leading south to the bank of the river above the Falls.

When part way there, they met a company of Indians coming down the Portage, with their packs on their backs and their canoes upside down over their heads.

"Where are you going?" asked Pierre. "To Fort Niagara?"

"No; we go on past there to Albany," was the reply. "The English there pay more for our furs."

"You are very late," said Pierre.

"Yes, we have come a long way, from the land of the Mississippi."

"Is that far?" asked Philippe.

"Almost a thousand miles," said Pierre.

"A thousand miles!" exclaimed Philippe. "All the way in canoes? Could they do that?"

"Oh, yes; that is often done."

Tall forest trees bordered the road on each side. The creaking carts went slowly along. Once in a while a deer appeared in the forest and went bounding off at the approach of the procession.

To Philippe, accustomed to a country that had fields and gardens and was dotted with villages, this was all new and exciting.

After three hours, as they neared the end of the road, Philippe could see some low wooden buildings, made of logs, surrounded by a stockade.

"Fort Little Niagara," Red Bird told him.

At the end of one of the buildings, he noticed a large chimney of rough stone.

There were Indian wigwams a short distance from the Fort. Most of the Indians were helping to carry packs on the Portage, but the Indian women were grinding corn and scraping skins around the wigwams, and Indian children were playing.

"Do Indians live here?" asked Philippe, in surprise.

"Not many," said Pierre. "These few and those you saw at the other end of the Portage are the only ones. The rest of the Seneca tribe live about a hundred miles east of here, but they control all the land between."

"Me Seneca," said Red Bird proudly. "My tribe Keepers of Western Door."

The carts were unloaded near the river bank and the Indians who had carried packs threw them down. The canoes were placed at the edge of the water, ready to be shoved in.

"Is the Commandant here? I want to give him the letter," said Philippe.

"I'll find out," Pierre replied.

In a few minutes he came back, saying, "Sieur Chabert is still away, but he is expected back tonight."

It was noon and the men were hungry. They

went into the building which had the big stone chimney that Philippe had noticed. This building was the barracks and mess-house, and in the kitchen the cook stood before the fireplace, getting the mid-day meal. With the money they earned carrying the loads up the Portage, many of the men bought rum to drink.

Pierre wanted the canoes loaded at once, so they could start on their way to Detroit. But the men, having drunk the rum, were stupid and wanted to sleep.

"Perhaps I had better humor them," said Pierre to the storekeeper. "It would not be safe to trust them with the canoes till they have slept it off."

"Best wait," said the storekeeper.

Pierre took the keg with the red stripe into the storehouse and placed it behind some bales of fur.

"Don't let anyone touch that keg," said Pierre. "I'll load it myself when I come back."

Then he turned to the boys. "I'll go down to the Falls with you now."

# CHAPTER VIII

## AT THE FALLS

S THEY left the Little Fort, the broad river at their left, a mile wide, flowed smoothly along, with never a projecting rock or streak of foam; but they had not gone far when the current was swifter and the surface became rough. Before long the water began to flow more sharply down hill and the rapids appeared. Over the rocky bed of the wide river the water boiled and swirled and leaped into the air, topped with lovely white foam. A beautiful sight it was, as it went dashing along, now breaking into spray against projecting rocks, again rushing madly on.

The three had come opposite an island, the one now called Goat Island, which divides the American from the Canadian or Horseshoe Falls. They stood on the bank under a willow tree whose limbs hung over the edge of the river, looking at the swirling, leaping waters.

"If a canoe should come down into these rapids, could it be saved?" asked Philippe.

"No," said Pierre. "There is no saving a boat that comes as far as this down the river."

"What happens to it?" asked Philippe.

"It is carried over the Falls and is dashed to pieces on the rocks below," said Pierre.

"Once big cask went over and came safe down to Fort," said Red Bird. "Me saw it."

"That might happen once in a while," admitted Pierre; "but usually anything that goes over the Falls is lost forever."

They walked along the bank to the very brink of the cataract, where the river makes a sharp turn to the right. At that point, so close that they could put out their hands and almost touch the rushing water as it poured over the edge, they stood and gazed at the wondrous sight.

Pierre and Red Bird had seen it many times, but to Philippe, seeing it for the first time, it was such a magnificent spectacle that he stood there spellbound. Not only was he lost in wonder at the madly rushing water, tumbling over the brink and striking the rocks nearly two hundred feet below with a deafening roar, but he was surprised at the white mist rising from the foot of the cataract, at the beautiful rainbow in the mist, and at the lovely colors of the water

—pale green, turning here to lavender and there to pink, all covered with lacy white spray.

His eyes roved along the brink of the American Falls, near which they were standing, past the wooded island a thousand feet away, to the curving Horseshoe Falls beyond. He had never imagined anything so grand.

"And the wonder is that it never stops," said Pierre. "Winter and summer I have been here, and it is always rushing over the brink with that same roar. And always the white mist is rising. It is one grand and beautiful sight."

Pierre and Red Bird were talking together, but Philippe continued to gaze at the marvelous view. Suddenly he became aware that Red Bird was shouting and pointing up the river.

"Look! Coming down rapids!" he was saying.

"A canoe!" exclaimed Pierre. "A canoe coming toward the Falls!"

"Oh!" exclaimed Philippe. "Is any one in it?"

"No one, I think," said Pierre.

It was still up the river a quarter of a mile. It rushed along, tossed about in the swirling currents, then stopped for a few seconds, as it was caught on a projecting rock, and went rushing on again.

"Alas!" said Pierre. "A good canoe will be

dashed to pieces. It is well there is nothing
in it."

It came nearer and nearer the brink of the
Falls.

"See! Something in it!" shouted Red Bird.

# AT THE FALLS

"A keg! A keg!" cried Philippe.

At that moment the keg rolled out of the canoe and went bobbing up and down in the water, tossed now here, now there.

"Red stripe on keg!" exclaimed Red Bird.

"My keg! The doll is lost!" declared Pierre.

The canoe came down faster and soon was opposite them and went rushing over the brink of the Falls and was lost to sight.

The keg soon came rolling and tumbling down toward the brink and was swept over the Falls.

"I shall never see it again," groaned Pierre. "The little Marie will have no doll from Paris to while away the long winter days."

"Maybe won't break," said Red Bird, consolingly. "Strong keg."

"Could it go over the Falls without being dashed to pieces?" asked Pierre. "Could it go safely through the whirlpool and the terrible rapids?"

"Maybe," said Red Bird. "Maybe we find down river."

"No; that will never happen," said Pierre. "It has already been dashed to pieces."

They started back to the Little Fort.

"Philippe and me, we watch for keg, down river," said Red Bird.

"It's no use," insisted Pierre.

"We watch," repeated Red Bird. "Tomorrow maybe we find; maybe next day."

Pierre smiled ruefully and said, "You are good friends of mine, you two."

As they were walking back, Philippe asked, "How do you suppose the keg came in the river?"

"We'll find out," answered Pierre. "Some one put it in."

When they arrived at the Fort, the men were standing in groups.

"How did the keg get into the river?" Pierre demanded.

"It was Antoine," said the storekeeper.

"I was sure of it," said Pierre.

"He came for it, saying he had orders to load it," said the storekeeper. "I thought it was the truth. I was busy and knew no more about it till the men came and told me."

"Where is that Antoine?" asked Pierre angrily.

"He started back toward Montreal," said one of the men. "He was afraid to stay and face Pierre."

"He is a scoundrel," said Pierre. "He has cheated a little girl of great joy, just to get even for an old grudge. Just let me catch that rogue sometime!"

In a few minutes they were all busy, loading the canoes for Detroit.

"You lads will stay here tonight," said Pierre, "and go down tomorrow with my friend François. Sieur de Chabert may come back. Then you can give him the letter, Philippe."

When the canoes were all loaded and ready to start on their long trip, Pierre said to the boys, "I'll be gone about three weeks. Adieu till then."

"Good-by, Pierre," they said.

"Be sure to come back," Philippe called, as the canoe started off.

The boys stood on the bank and watched the fleet, as it went out into the river and turned upstream. They watched till the canoes had gone out of sight on the far side of Grand Island, on their way to Lake Erie. They saw a flock of geese flying south, high in the sky. They watched seagulls circling over the river. They threw pieces of wood as far into the river as they could throw, and watched them carried by the current downstream.

"Maybe they go over Falls," said Red Bird.

When they were tired of doing that, they went into the storehouse and watched the trading of a band of Indians who had come with furs to sell.

Philippe looked on with interest, as they held up skins of the beaver or the fox and pointed to the things they wanted. He noticed that they were not satisfied, and finally went away without doing much trading.

"Why didn't they buy things?" he asked the storekeeper.

"They say we do not pay enough for their furs, so they will take them to Oswego or Albany, to the English, who give more."

"Those places are a long way off," said Philippe.

"Yes, but they do not care. They will slip past Fort Niagara in the night. Those English are getting much of our trade away."

"Is Sieur de Chabert coming tonight?" asked Philippe, at bedtime.

"We think he will come, but he may be late," said the storekeeper. "You two lads may sleep on those bales of furs."

They were glad to go to bed early, after the long exciting day, and were soon fast asleep.

# CHAPTER IX

## THE BIG STONE CHIMNEY

IEUR DE CHABERT returned late that night, and early the next morning he asked that Philippe be brought to him. He received the boy kindly, saying, "So you are the son of Captain de Croix?"

"Yes, *Monsieur le Commandant.*"

"I am glad you came. Your father is a good friend of mine and a fine soldier. You should be proud."

"I am, sir. I have a letter for you, from him."

"This is most important," said the Commandant, when he had finished reading it. "It gives information that will be valuable to me and to the cause of France. You may come back in half an hour for an answer."

As he and Red Bird strolled among the buildings inside the stockade, they came to the big chimney Philippe had noticed as they arrived at the Fort.

"What a big, strong chimney!" said Philippe.

It was made of rough stone, gathered there in the neighborhood, and had been built sturdy and true, a few years before. Little did the boys think that it would still be standing nearly two hundred years afterward, though more than once the building to which it belonged would be burned to the ground. Little did they think that it would serve to warm the soldiers of three nations, France, Great Britain and the United States.

The boys next went to the landing and watched a small fleet of canoes that was coming in sight up the river. It proved to be a band of Indians from an Ohio tribe, with their women, their boys and girls and their papooses. They had come to spend the winter near Fort Niagara.

"Why do they do that?" asked Philippe.

"So as to be fed during the winter," said the soldier on guard.

Having a little more time, the boys ran a few rods along the bank of the river and watched a water wheel that was running a crude sawmill.

When Philippe returned to the Commandant, Sieur Chabert said, "Here is a letter for your father. Be careful that it does not fall into the hands of any one else."

"I'll be careful," Philippe promised.

"I'll tell you one of the things it contains, so

if by chance it should be lost, you can tell your father. He wished to know whether the Seneca Indians are remaining true to the French. I have just been among them. I go there often and can speak their language. I find out their plans

and feelings, because I have been adopted into their tribe. They are still loyal to us."

"But you are not an Indian, are you?" asked Philippe.

"No; I am French, the son of Joncaire, who lived here on the Niagara for forty years. He also was adopted by the Senecas and did a great work for France by securing their friendship. His cabin was at the foot of the Portage Hill.

It was he who obtained their permission to build the Castle at Fort Niagara."

Sieur Chabert was silent for a few moments, while Philippe waited, hoping for something more. Finally he repeated, "Yes, the Senecas are still on our side."

"Then which ones are against us?" asked Philippe.

"I'll explain to you. The Iroquois Indians are divided into five Nations—the Mohawks, the Onondagas, the Oneidas, the Cayugas and the Senecas. About forty years ago, the Tuscaroras came up from the south and joined them, so now there are really Six Nations. The Mohawks live farthest east, toward Albany, the Senecas farthest west, and the others between. The Senecas are our friends. The Mohawks are friends of the English. Sir William Johnson, who lives near Albany, is friendly with them, as I am with the Senecas. We are not so sure about the other tribes. Sometimes they seem friendly to us, sometimes to the English."

"I wish there were no war going on," exclaimed Philippe.

"So do I, lad, so do I; but are we to let the English settle in our territory and take all the fur trade? They now offer more for furs than we can, so that much of the trade is going to them. No; we'll do our best to hold this great river and portage for King Louis."

It was the very thing Pierre had said. It was what the officers at Fort Niagara had said.

"Your father is a fine man, Philippe. I can wish nothing better for you than to follow in his footsteps. Now you and Red Bird may go down the Portage with François and his band. Don't go off by yourselves."

"We'll be sure to keep with François, sir," said Philippe.

The two boys joined the company that was starting down the Portage. They walked the eight miles along the Portage Road, then down the long, steep hill, the men carrying the canoes and packs. Then they put their canoes in the river and paddled down to the Fort.

As they glided along between the beautiful forest-covered banks, the two boys kept turning their heads this way and that, as if watching for something.

"What are you looking for?" asked François.

"Pierre's keg," replied Philippe.

"It would not go over the Falls without breaking."

"It might," said Red Bird.

"Anyway, it would not come down so soon. Tomorrow, maybe; or next day. Sometimes a thing that has gone over the Falls, goes round and round in the whirlpool for days, before getting out of it and going on down the river."

"We watch," declared Red Bird.

"I wish you luck," said François.

In a few minutes, Philippe exclaimed, "Oh! What is that dark thing over there?"

"Might be keg," said Red Bird.

They both watched eagerly, as the canoe changed its course in order to come nearer.

"I believe it is the keg," said Philippe, as they approached it.

"You boys imagine things," said François. "That is only a short log."

"Oh, yes," admitted Philippe, when they came nearer.

They arrived at Fort Niagara in time for dinner.

The baker called to Red Bird as they passed the bake-house, "I am glad you are back. No one can light the fires as well as you."

Red Bird grinned.

When Philippe gave the note to his father, he said, "Oh, Father, Pierre's keg went over the Falls."

"Went over the Falls! How did that happen?"

Philippe told him and added, "Pierre feels terribly sad because the little girl in Detroit will be disappointed."

"I am sorry for Pierre," said Captain de Croix. "He had set his heart on getting it there safe."

# CHAPTER X

## CAPTIVES

HAT evening, just after dusk, Philippe went over to the main gate of the Fort, for he liked to see the drawbridge pulled up. This gate, which opened onto the Portage Road, had been named "The Gate of the Five Nations," after the five tribes of the Iroquois Indians. Sometimes they came bringing furs to trade; sometimes on a friendly visit; sometimes to make a treaty with the French; sometimes to beg food and presents. Sometimes they came bringing scalps and captives.

The drawbridge, which extended over the moat, was raised at night or in time of danger, so no enemy could come suddenly into the Fort. The heavy wooden doors were closed and fastened with huge bolts.

Philippe had come just in time, for two soldiers, one on each side, were turning the windlasses that raised the drawbridge. On each side, high in the air, was a huge stone for a counterweight. As the windlasses were turned and wound up the heavy ropes, the stones descended. With much creaking, the bridge was pulled up against the entrance of the Fort.

The bridge had been raised, the big doors had been closed and bolted; and Philippe had just started over to the Castle for the night, when there was a great shouting and whooping across the moat.

"A band of Indians!" said one of the soldiers on guard. "They can't come in now."

"Of course not," said another. "The bridge is up for the night. They will have to wait till morning."

The shouting and the whooping kept up. With insistent calls the Indians demanded to be admitted.

"Run to the Castle and tell the Commandant," said the guard to Philippe. "We won't let them in without orders."

Philippe ran across the parade ground to the Castle. Soon he was back at the gate, with one of the officers.

"The orders are to admit them if there are only a few," said the officer.

"There are five and some captives," said the guard.

They let the drawbridge down and the Indians filed across. Their painted faces made them look frightful. Hanging from the belts of three of them were scalps. With them were two captives—a man of forty and a young man of about twenty. They were English and seemed to be farmers.

A guard of soldiers led them across the parade ground to a room on the first floor of the Castle, where the Commandant was waiting to receive them.

"Where did you get these captives?" he asked.

"In the Susquehanna Country," said the leader.

"We'll keep them here," said the Commandant.

"No; we want," said the leader.

"We'll give you fine presents for them."

"No; we no give up. We keep," said one of the Indians.

The Commandant spoke in an undertone to an officer: "Bring some presents. We'll buy the captives."

When the officer returned, the Commandant picked up a fine big blanket. "We will give this for the older man," he said.

"No; we no give up," insisted the leader.

"We'll give two blankets and many beads."

"No; we take to our tribe."

Then the Commandant took some money, ten livres, from his wallet and held it out.

"We give much money," he said.

The Indians consulted together for a few minutes. Then the leader spoke: "We take money. Man stay."

He was informed of his good luck and passed over to the side of the French officers.

Then the Commandant said, "We'll give much for the young man. We'll give three blankets and six knives and many beads."

The leader shook his head.

"We keep," he said sternly.

"We'll give money," the Commandant offered. He held out some gold pieces.

"No; our Chief's son died. This young man fine and strong. He be our Chief's son."

All the while the young man stood silent, realizing well enough what was being said. Philippe was sorry for him and wondered why he did not speak to the Commandant and beg to be rescued. He sadly watched the young man go out of the Castle with the Indians; then he went upstairs with his father.

"Where are the Indians going to take that captive?" he asked.

"They will take him to live with the tribe," replied Captain de Croix.

"Will he ever be allowed to go back to his home?"

"No; probably not. He will have to live there all his life."

"Why didn't he speak to the officers and beg to be rescued?"

"That would only have made matters worse. The Indians might have quickly struck him down with their tomahawks, if he had made the slightest effort to get away."

"Then why didn't you officers just take him away from the Indians?"

"If we had tried to take him by force, he would almost surely have been killed instantly. The savages will not be interfered with. We officers knew that."

"It must be terrible to be captured by Indians," said Philippe, after a few moments.

"It *is* terrible," his father agreed.

# CHAPTER XI

## THE KEG

HE next morning the boys went early to the water's edge and watched all the forenoon to see if the keg would come drifting down. A soldier, off duty, said to them, "What are you boys doing?"

"We are watching for a keg that went over the Falls," replied Philippe.

"That is a queer thing to look for," said the soldier.

"There is something nice in it," said Philippe.

"Keg went over two days ago," said Red Bird.

"Perhaps it has gone past already," said the soldier. "It probably has, if it didn't get smashed to pieces. It may have floated down in the night."

But the boys stayed there patiently all the forenoon and looked eagerly over the water at every passing bit of drift. A few things went floating past, but no keg.

In the afternoon Red Bird said, "We go out in canoe. See better that way."

Philippe liked very much to go canoeing. As they pushed out into the river, he wished he could handle a canoe as deftly as Red Bird, whose every stroke seemed to send the boat in just the right direction.

"How did you learn to do it so well?" he asked.

"Paddled long time. When only seven, me paddle canoe much."

Try as hard as he could to dip the paddle as Red Bird showed him, Philippe could not quite do it.

"Red Bird is skillful," he thought. How different was his opinion of the Indian boy from the one he had formed that first night!

They started upstream, keeping near the east bank. On all the broad river, theirs was the only canoe that afternoon.

On both the west side and the east side, the forest came to the bank of the river, so the blue water flowed between gorgeous banks of red and gold and green. The ripples sparkled in the sunshine that autumn day.

All at once Philippe exclaimed, "What is that, off there in the water?"

"We find out," said Red Bird, as he hurried the canoe up the river.

The dark object went bobbing along, now taken by an eddy nearer shore, now carried by a current away from the shore.

They went nearer, Philippe's keen eyes watching as Red Bird paddled the canoe.

"I think it is only a log," he said, as they came nearer. In a few moments, however, he shouted, "A keg! A keg!"

Red Bird paddled faster. "Pierre's keg," he cried, as they reached it.

"Oh, no; it has no red stripe," said Philippe.

"Maybe paint wash off," said Red Bird.

In a few moments, Philippe cried, "Some of the paint is still there! It *is* Pierre's!"

Philippe reached over the side and touched it, but it quickly bobbed away. In trying to grasp it, he nearly capsized the canoe.

"Have care!" said Red Bird.

Again he brought the canoe up to it. Once more, as Philippe's hand touched the rounding surface of the slippery keg, it floated off.

"I can't get it that way," he said. "I'll push it with the paddle."

He placed his paddle against it in such a way as to hold it against the side of the canoe.

"See! It is whole," he shouted.

They had gone up the river nearly a mile. The current would help them going back; but an undercurrent might whisk the keg away at any moment. Philippe found it no easy task to hold the keg in place with his paddle.

Once when he reached over too far and tipped the canoe, he nearly went into the river, and he *did* lose his paddle. The keg went in one direction, the paddle in another.

"Oh, now we'll never get that keg to shore," said he.

"We try more," said Red Bird.

With a few strokes he sent the canoe within reach of the paddle, but then the keg was several rods away, going down the river.

It looked as though they might have to give up; but again Red Bird sent the canoe forward with swift strokes and they overtook the keg. Again Philippe placed his paddle against it and pushed it along.

They had brought it within a few rods of the landing, where some Indians and soldiers were standing, watching them. Among them was Sergeant La Barre.

"Plucky boys," said he.

Suddenly a current whisked it away again. Philippe leaned over to catch it and tumbled head foremost into the water. In an instant, Red Bird had jumped after him and they both disappeared from sight in the deep water.

"To the rescue!" exclaimed Sergeant La Barre. "The current is strong there."

He leaped to a canoe; one of the Indians got in with him. They started out, paddling the canoe with swift strokes toward the spot where the boys had gone down.

Red Bird came to the surface and began to swim toward shore as soon as he saw that the men would look after Philippe, who had been under the water longer and had to be lifted into the canoe and brought ashore.

Meanwhile, another Indian had gone after the keg and brought it in.

It was a few minutes before Philippe came to consciousness. His first question was, "Is the keg safe?"

"Yes," replied Sergeant La Barre. "It is all safe. But why did you boys take all that trouble and risk your lives for a keg? What is in it?"

"That is Pierre's keg, the one he brought up from Montreal," said Philippe. "Hadn't you heard that it went over the Falls?"

"No; but is it the same one? There is not much red paint on this one."

"It wash off," said Red Bird.

"It is lucky you were near shore when you fell in," said the Sergeant.

"But we had to get it," said Philippe.

The boys carried it between them up to the Fort and through the small gate. The Chaplain met them as they were going to the Castle.

"What is that you are carrying so carefully?" he asked.

"Pierre's keg," said Philippe. "It is the one that went over the Falls."

"And you boys found it!" exclaimed Father Joseph.

"Yes," said Red Bird, "we find in river."

"What a miracle that it came over the Falls without being smashed!" said Father Joseph.

They went on and took the keg to Philippe's room, to stay till Pierre should return.

Captain de Croix was told of the incident by Sergeant La Barre.

"Plucky lads they were," he said, "but it was a risky thing to do."

When Philippe and his father were talking that evening, Captain de Croix said, "It was a rash thing that you and Red Bird did, in trying to get the keg to shore."

"But we had to do it," declared Philippe. "Could we let Pierre's keg float out into the lake and be lost?"

"No; you did right. It was rash, but I would much prefer that my son be brave and useful than that he should always weigh the chances for safety."

# CHAPTER XII

## THE DEPARTURE

WO weeks later Philippe and his father were in their room one evening, talking over many things. After a few minutes Philippe said, "Please put on your gold-laced coat, Father. I like to see you in it."

"Of course, son. Hand it to me."

Philippe took the coat from its peg and held it toward his father, who put it on.

"You look just as you did on my birthday, the year before you came to America," said Philippe. "Didn't I think you were splendid then?"

"Did you?" asked Captain de Croix with a smile.

"Yes, the coat was so gay that it helped to give me the grandest time. I remember thinking I would have one just like it when I grew up. You gave me my watch that year. Don't you remember?"

"Was that the year?"

"Yes; and I never look at the watch without seeing you in your gold-laced coat. It was a great comfort when you were away. That is why I brought it along."

"I hope it will always bring you pleasant memories," said the Captain.

The candle sent flickering lights and shadows over their faces and over the gleaming coat.

Philippe's mother had died when he was a small boy. He could only dimly remember her as a beautiful lady who had been gracious in manner and lovely to look on. He and his father had been close companions all these years till Captain de Croix came to America, two years before. These evening talks together were enjoyed by both of them the more, because they had long been separated.

"I don't see why our King wants to fight for this country," said Philippe. "There is nothing but forest in it. Why does King Louis want so much forest?"

"Every king wants as much territory as he can get, my son. This land may bring in great profit some day, for its forests are full of fur-bearing animals."

"I know. Pierre told me," said Philippe. "All winter long the trappers are busy catching the beaver, the fox, the otter and other animals. In the spring the canoes bring the furs down the rivers and lakes to the trading posts and exchange them for goods."

"Yes; the fur trade is one reason for our wishing to keep New France. There is another reason, also. Our great explorers discovered this part of America. They explored it at great danger to themselves and at great cost. Champlain, Marquette, Joliet, Cartier and La Salle were the first to go into many parts of New France. Shall we let go what they, at such a great price, brought to France? La Salle passed up and down this Niagara several times. He climbed that Portage Hill. He built the first fort on the Niagara. He built a ship to sail on the Great Lakes, a few miles above Fort Little Niagara, where you went. Shall I not be willing to help keep what he brought to France?"

He turned to his desk to write a letter.

Philippe went to the map of deerskin that hung on the wall and again followed with his finger the route a canoe would take, up the Portage, past Little Niagara, up Lake Erie to Presque Isle, and to the other forts south and west of there. Then he started again at Fort Little Niagara and followed the shore of Lake Erie along to Detroit, where Pierre had gone.

When his father had finished the letter, Philippe asked, "Is it very dangerous here? Are there any English near?"

"I have something to tell you," said Captain de Croix. "That is the very thing our Commandant wants to find out. The scouts that have been sent have not always given us correct information, so he wishes two of us to go on a scouting trip toward Fort Oswego, to find out whether the English are there and how many of them. He wishes me to go."

"You? Oh, no, Father, not you."

"I must go," replied Captain de Croix. "We start early tomorrow morning."

"But, Father, that is dangerous."

"Philippe, would you wish me to shirk duty, even when it is dangerous?"

"That would not be like you," Philippe replied.

"No; I cannot. The Commandant has asked me to go. I shall do my best to find out what he wants to know."

"But tomorrow morning! That is so soon."

"I know; I had wished to be with you longer. But this is war. I must do my part."

"But you must come back," cried Philippe, after a moment of silence.

"I shall try," was the reply. "I shall go disguised. A trusty Seneca is to be my guide."

Early the next morning, in the light of the flickering candle, Philippe wakened to see his father, dressed in the deerskin garments of a Seneca, standing by his bed.

"I am starting, Philippe," he said. "Whatever happens, always be brave, be true and, above all, be kind."

"I'll try, Father; but you will come back, won't you?"

"I hope to," responded Captain de Croix. "I'll always be on the watch for danger. Good-by, my son."

"Good-by," said Philippe, with tears in his eyes.

The door opened and closed.

In the stillness of the early morning, Philippe could hear the dull roar of the Falls.

# CHAPTER XIII

## BELTS OF WAMPUM

FTEN a band of Indians came through the Gate of the Five Nations to have a Council with the Commandant at Fort Niagara, Captain de Vassan, or to make a treaty. In their gorgeous costumes of beaded garments and headdresses, each with its single eagle plume, they would be conducted across the parade ground to the Room of the Commandant in the Castle. Always they brought belts of wampum to use in these ceremonies.

Wampum was made from shells formed into beads, with a hole in the center for stringing. It was used as money among the Indians and among many of the early white settlers. It was used in keeping the records of the tribe. It was also used in making a treaty, when belts were passed back and forth to make a record of the things said and to help the parties to remember the promises made.

Wampum was of two colors, white and purple. Each belt had a meaning, according to the number of rows and the design woven in it.

Two days after Captain de Croix went away, a deputation of Seneca Indians came through the Gate of the Five Nations. A dozen of the old men of the tribe came first and a number of the young warriors followed, in single file.

"Come to see Big Chief," said the leader.

Some of the guard took them across the parade ground to the Castle. Philippe was in the front entrance room at the time. He followed as they entered the Room of the Commandant, where, a little later, Captain de Vassan and his staff came.

"You will have to leave now," one of the guard said to Philippe.

"Let the lad stay," said the Commandant. "He will be interested in this ceremony."

Silent and grave, the Indians sat, waiting for the Commandant to begin. Dignified and erect, the French staff sat, in their brilliant uniforms. The peace pipe was lighted by the Chief, and passed to the Commandant, who took two or three puffs and passed it along, till it had gone to all in the Council.

The Commandant rose and began:

"I thank the Great Spirit that he has permitted our brothers, the Senecas, to come to Fort Niagara. They are most welcome. They are a brave tribe. The Sun never shone on young men who were better warriors and old men who were greater in wisdom. May the stars of many nights shine on the friendship between the French and the Senecas. With this belt I renew the Covenant-Chain between us. Since it was made, it has never once slipped or broken. It has always been kept bright and clean, without any stain or rust. We who represent King Louis of France will make sure that it remain so, as long as the Sun and the Moon shall endure."

He then passed a belt of wampum to the leader of the Senecas.

The spokesman for them arose and replied:

"We come from the tribe of the Senecas, to seal our friendship with the French and with our great Father, King Louis of France. We have come four days' march along the trail, through forest and swamp, to see our brothers, the French, and to talk of important things. May the path always be kept open between us."

He handed a fine belt of wampum to the Commandant, as a pledge that his words were true.

The Commandant spoke again:

"The hearts of the French are heavy and their eyes weep tears for any sorrows that have come to their brothers, the Senecas, during past moons. We pray that the Great Spirit will take good care of their warriors, their women and their children who have departed from this life. With this belt we wipe away the tears from their eyes."

He handed a belt of purple wampum, the sign of mourning.

After a few moments of silence, the spokesman solemnly replied:

"The Senecas are grateful to their brothers, the French, for their kind thoughts toward those of our tribe who have departed. They wish that the Sun may ever shine on the cornfields of the French, and that the Moon may bring good luck to all their undertakings."

As a seal to this, he again passed a belt of wampum.

The Commandant felt that the Indians had not yet stated the real purpose of their visit, so he said, "We ask our brothers, the Senecas, to name their desires. Since they are our friends, we will give them presents and send them home with joy in their hearts."

Once more he passed a belt of wampum as a pledge of his sincerity.

The leader replied:

"The English give many gifts to those who fight on their side. Our brothers, the Mohawks and the Oneidas and the Onondagas and the Cayugas, get big presents. They come back to their villages laden with fine clothing and many

beads, with blankets and knives, with bright
cloth for their women and necklaces for their
maidens. They bring gold-laced coats, very
fine. Sir William Johnson, the friend of the
Mohawks, has offered us many presents if we
will fight on the side of the English."

The Commandant replied:

"We will be true to our brothers, the Senecas,
and will keep the road open, so that they may
continue to come back and forth. We wish our
brothers, the Senecas, to have as fine gifts as the
Mohawks. We will give many blankets and
beads, kettles and guns, powder and shot, bright
ribbons for the young maidens, bright red cloth
from which the Seneca women can make clothes.
I give this belt of wampum as a seal of our true
friendship and our love for the Senecas."

He extended a wide belt of white wampum.

He turned to two of his staff and asked them
to place the gifts on the table.

The eyes of the Indians gleamed with satis-
faction, when they saw the array of gifts.

The leader spoke again:

"Now we know that the French are indeed
our brothers. Our young warriors will go on
the warpath for the great King Louis. Our old
men will advise the tribe to be true to the French.
As the corn grows strong in the season of the new
Moon, may the strength of our brothers, the

French, increase, till they drive the English out of the borders of their lands."

He handed the Commandant a wide belt of wampum.

The Commandant answered:

"We thank our brothers, the Senecas, for their help and their good wishes. We invite them to sit down to a feast, in order that they may be cheered and refreshed, before they take the trail homeward. This belt is given this day to confirm the treaty between the great tribe of the Senecas and the great King of France, Louis the

Fifteenth, and his soldiers at Fort Niagara. The Council fire is covered."

He handed a wide belt of wampum to the leader.

The visitors were led to the great kitchen and seated at the long table, where they were served all the food they could eat, salt pork from Montreal, bread baked in the big ovens, molasses and raisins, and a pudding made by the cook.

As they finished and were about to leave, the Commandant once more addressed them:

"Our brothers are invited to come again. The Great White Father, King Louis, will keep the trail open for them to come back and forth to Fort Niagara. He will give them supplies of food and guns. He will give good prices for their furs. May they have good hunting and a safe journey to their villages."

The Senecas took the belts of wampum that had been given them and departed with their many gifts.

# CHAPTER XIV

## AN OCTOBER DAY

ACH morning Philippe saw the gold-laced coat when first he opened his eyes. Each evening it was the last thing on which his eyes rested. Almost a week had passed and he often wondered when his father would come back.

Strolling here and there to pass the time one morning, he found Red Bird coming out of the bake-house after lighting the fire. They went over to the gunsmith's cabin and watched him work.

"It seems as if these guns are always getting broken," he said. "We must have every gun in working order if an attack comes unexpectedly."

"It won't come this fall, will it?" asked Philippe.

"How do I know, lad? How do I know? I wish it would never come, but there are rumors. The trouble is we can't depend on what our Indian scouts tell us."

Philippe wanted to say that his father had

gone and would surely find out the truth; then he thought that perhaps he had better not tell of it. The two boys watched while the gunsmith placed a piece of iron in the fire. They pumped the bellows for him. They liked to hear the blows of the hammer on the red-hot iron, to see the sparks that flew from it, and to hear the hissing sound that came when the hot iron was plunged into the cask of water standing near by.

From the gunsmith's cabin, they went to the lake shore and walked along the narrow, pebbly beach, toward the east, stopping to skip stones over the smooth water now and then. The ripples, glinting in the sunlight, made the surface of the lake sparkle and gleam like a multitude of jewels.

A walk of four miles brought them to the mouth of a creek that flows into the lake. On each side of the creek there was low ground called "The Little Marsh," where all sorts of wild creatures lived in the muddy waters. Next summer this creek and marsh were to become famous, but today there was not much in sight but a flock of wild ducks that had alighted on the creek, if one did not count some dark objects sitting in a row on a log.

The boys did count them. "There are six," said Philippe. "Let's catch one and take it back to the Fort."

"Must be very still," whispered Red Bird.

The boys stepped softly through the shallow water. The six dark objects might have been made of wood, so motionless were they.

When almost there, each boy reached out to grab one. Alas, they were gone! The six turtles had slipped quietly but very swiftly off the log into the water and were out of sight.

Red Bird grinned. "They always do that," he said. "They wise."

The flock of wild ducks, hearing the sound of voices, rose into the air and flew away. The two boys were on the bank of the little creek, with the woods and the marsh spread out around them. Off to the north, the water of the lake was blue under a blue October sky. The October sunshine lay soft around them.

"Let's go up the creek," said Philippe.

They started up the winding stream, but had gone only around the first bend when Red Bird stooped and picked up a stone.

"Oh! A hammerstone," he said.

"A what?" asked Philippe.

"A hammerstone. See hollows in it."

It was a round thick stone, with a little hollow on each side.

"What is it for?" asked Philippe.

"Crack nuts."

Red Bird placed his thumb in the hollow on

one side of the stone and a finger in the hollow on the other side. He walked a few steps into the woods and found a hickory nut, which he placed on a big log and cracked with the hammerstone.

"See," said he.

"I see," said Philippe. "I wish I had one."

They searched all around but could not find another.

"Where did it come from?" asked Philippe.

"One of Iroquois dropped it. Maybe Seneca. Maybe Mohawk."

"Oh! Is any one near us now?" asked Philippe.

"Better go back to Fort," said Red Bird.

They lost no time in hurrying along the beach toward the Fort, only stopping three or four times to skip a stone across the water.

"In winter, ice all over this water," said Red Bird, as they hurried along.

Philippe made no answer, for he was thinking of something else. He was thinking what fun he and Red Bird could have, exploring that creek and other places in this part of the country, if only there were no enemies lurking around.

# CHAPTER XV

S THE boys came toward the Castle, a group of officers, standing in front of the door, were engaged in conversation. Philippe felt that they were talking about him and wondered what they were saying.

"Who will tell him?" one of them asked.

"It will not be an easy thing to do," said Captain Du Charme.

"No, it will not," said Lieutenant Le Maire. "He and his father were unusually devoted to each other."

"Father Joseph will do it. Where is he?" said the Captain.

But they were all relieved from the unpleasant duty. Red Bird went up to them and asked, "What trouble?"

"Bad news has come. Captain de Croix has been killed."

"Killed!" exclaimed Red Bird. "Oh, me sorry for Philippe."

"No one wishes to tell him."

"Me tell," said Red Bird.

He went back to Philippe and said, in the words he had heard many a time, "The Great Spirit has taken your father."

"Taken my father!" exclaimed Philippe.

"Yes, he gone where all great warriors go, to Happy Hunting Grounds."

Philippe understood only too well what Red Bird meant. He had heard him, only the other day, use those same words about a great Indian Chief. He ran up to the group and asked, "What happened to him?"

"A runner has come with news that he was killed by a Mohawk when about half way to Oswego."

Philippe stood silent, as if stunned. Then he burst into weeping.

"Captain de Croix was a brave man," said Captain Du Charme. "There was none braver or more loved among the officers here at Fort Niagara. We'll give him a soldier's burial."

"Is he to be brought back?" asked Philippe.

"Yes, four of them are on the way, four Senecas who have often been here and knew him."

Philippe wanted to be alone; so he went over to the Lombardy poplars, where he could look out over the blue water of the lake and think.

He thought of his father, as he was starting

so gallantly off for America, two years before, to fight for New France; he thought of their joyous meeting just a few weeks ago; he thought of their happy evenings together here at the Fort. Then he sobbed again at the thought that they would never have such evenings again.

Red Bird had stayed back near the Castle, but now it seemed to him that Philippe needed him; so he went up quietly and sat down near him.

No words were spoken, but Philippe was comforted by his friendly presence.

Two days later a military funeral was held in the little chapel in the Castle. The banner of France covered the coffin in which Philippe's father lay.

That evening, when Philippe went up to bed, the beautiful coat cheered up the dim room. It helped to take his sadness away, for it brought back to his mind the picture of his father, saying, "My son, whatever befalls you, be brave, be true and, above all, be kind."

# CHAPTER XVI

## ABIGAIL WENTWORTH

BOUT this time in the eastern part of the Province of New York, not far west of Albany, Abigail Wentworth sat by the window of the large sitting room, doing her daily stint of sewing. She was piecing together squares of bright calicoes for a bedquilt. There was a pucker in Abbie's pretty forehead. Finally she broke out with, "Oh, dear! Why does this thread have to bother me so?"

"What is the trouble?" asked her mother, who, at the opposite window, was working some beautiful embroidery.

"There is a knot in my thread. I wanted to get my stint done, so I could go over to see Lydia's new dress."

"I'll help to get it out," said Mother.

With the needle in it, Abbie handed over the block she was piecing. Mrs. Wentworth not only got the knot out but, pulling the thread over and over between her fingers, straightened it so it would not twist again.

"Have you forgotten what I told you about getting the kinks out before starting to sew?" asked Mother kindly.

"I was in a hurry, so I thought I wouldn't take the time," said Abbie.

"The longest way round is often the shortest way home," said Mother, in a gentle voice. "You would have gained time by straightening the thread first."

"I s'pose so," admitted Abbie.

The room in which they were sitting was a large pleasant one, with a fireplace on one side. It had windows on the east and on the west and contained handsome furniture of mahogany.

The house was a large one of stone, set on a little hill. When Abbie's father received this large grant of land, Mrs. Wentworth had not wished, at first, to go so far away from the city of Albany; but after the fine large house was built, with the beautiful yard and gardens, she had come willingly and had never regretted it. Abbie's big brother was attending college at Yale. Abbie herself had a governess who taught her writing and French and many other interesting things.

The only other family near there were the Martins, who lived down the road. Lydia

Martin and Abbie were of the same age—ten. They went back and forth almost every day, to play or to do their stint of sewing together.

"May I go now, Mother?" asked Abbie, when she had finished the block.

"Yes; but don't stay long. It is nearing sunset."

Abbie started to get her cloak and hood, but turned and asked, "Oh, Mother, may I wear my best dress? Lydia is to put on her new one from New York for me to see. I'd like to wear my pink silk, so I shall be dressed up, too."

Mrs. Wentworth considered a moment. Why not let her wear it? The girls did not have many opportunities to wear their best dresses.

She replied, "Yes, you may wear it, but be careful not to tear it or get a spot on it."

"I'll be careful," Abbie promised. "May I wear my best slippers, too?"

"You couldn't walk over there in your thin slippers. Wear your everyday shoes and carry your slippers. You can put them on when you get there."

A few minutes later Abbie appeared, dressed in the pink silk, with sturdy shoes on her feet and the slippers in her hand.

"Abbie, if you are not home before sunset, do not start alone. I will send William over to walk home with you."

William was a trusted servant who had been with the family for many years.

"I'll wait, Mother."

Mrs. Wentworth watched with a smile as Abbie went gaily out of the yard and turned down the road toward the Martins' house, only one field away. She glanced up at the trees in the yard, the huge maples and elms that had been left standing when the land was cleared, now shedding their leaves of red and gold. She thought what a fine place this was for a home. Besides Abbie, there was her brother Charles, who was away at college, and a small sister, Sally. Grandmother and Grandfather also lived there.

Mr. Wentworth often had to be away on business, but there was always the servant, William, and several men who did the work of the farm. There was Emeline, the cook, and Anna, the maid. There was the governess, Mademoiselle Julie.

Mrs. Wentworth was alone with her thoughts as she went on with her embroidery. In half an hour, Grandmother and Grandfather came in from their room to sit by the fire.

"Where is Abbie?" asked Grandmother.

"She has gone over to see Lydia," was the reply.

"Isn't it about time she came home?" asked Grandmother.

"She'll be here soon," replied Mother.

"Abbie is getting big enough to take care of herself," said Grandfather. "She's bright, Abbie is."

"Yes, she is almost eleven," said Mother. "We must have a nice party on her birthday."

"Next month, isn't it?" asked Grandmother.

"Yes, next month."

The sun set behind the woods, yet Abbie had not come. Mrs. Wentworth pulled the bell-cord that hung by the door, and William answered the summons.

"You must go over to the Martins' and get Abbie. I don't wish her to walk home alone."

"Yes, Mrs. Wentworth."

He had not been gone long when the maid

came to the door in excitement and said, "Indians have been seen lurking around, down past the settlement. Peter Brown just came with the news."

"Indians!" exclaimed Grandmother. "I wish William and Abbie were back."

"The Indians probably won't come near us," said Grandfather. "That is five or six miles away."

Mrs. Wentworth looked anxiously out of the window in the direction of the Martins', but in the gathering darkness could not see anything of William.

She pulled the bell-cord again. "Fasten all the doors and windows," she said to the maid. "Then light the candles."

This was done and the three still sat talking before the fire. Then, quite suddenly, the cook came rushing in, saying, "Indians! I saw one go past the window toward the front of the house!"

"An Indian! Are you sure?"

"They cannot set the house on fire," said Grandmother. "It is made of stone."

"But Abbie! I hope she and William haven't left the Martins'," said Mrs. Wentworth.

She went to one of the windows and peered out around the curtain. All was still.

"There is no one in sight," she said.

The four looked at each other with anxious faces.

"Are you sure you saw some one?" she asked the cook.

The words were no sooner uttered than there was a scream in the front yard. Then all was quiet again.

"Oh! Oh!" cried Grandmother. Mrs. Wentworth went deadly white.

One of the farm hands came rushing in. "Indians!" he whispered hoarsely.

"Abbie!" said Mrs. Wentworth. "Abbie and William."

The man grabbed the gun that always stood by the door and went out into the yard. Soon he came running back and reported:

"William! He is dead there in the road."

"Heaven help us!" cried Mrs. Wentworth. "And Abbie! Where is she?"

No one tried to answer her question. They had little doubt.

But Grandmother, in the hope that it might be true, said, "Maybe she stayed at the Martins'. They may have heard of the Indian raid and kept her there."

"I'll find out," said the man.

He ran down the road, but was back in a few minutes.

"They say that William and Abbie started home together."

"Then Abbie has been carried off," said Mrs. Wentworth. She sank to the floor in a faint.

They lifted her to the couch and fanned her. In a few minutes the fainting spell passed and she sat up.

"This will not do," she said. "Quick! Saddle the horses and ride to the neighbors! They may be able to overtake the Indians."

Two of the farm men set out to carry the news to the settlers in all that section. They went on horseback to the nearest houses and said, "Abbie Wentworth has been carried off by Indians."

Then they came back and began a search that lasted till morning. Men came from the country around, as the news spread, to help in the search. But the forest stretched far toward the west. They found no trace of her but a tiny piece of pink silk hanging to a thorn a mile away. The forest had swallowed her up.

The next day Abbie's father came home. For days he and other men of the neighborhood searched the forest, going far toward the west.

It was a sad household that fall. Mrs. Wentworth tried to be brave for her husband's sake, and he tried to be brave for her sake; but they could not put Abbie out of their minds.

"If only I knew what has become of her," said

Mrs. Wentworth, more than once. "If only I knew whether she is living or dead, I could endure it better."

"These are troublous times for the colonists here on the border," said Grandfather. "When I was a boy we were always in dread of the Indians coming and killing some of us or carrying us off. I hoped we had seen the last of such doings."

"This war has made it worse again," said Mr. Wentworth. "The Indians on the side of the English go clear up toward Montreal to take French captives. War is a dreadful thing."

"As long as she was not killed, as William was, there is some hope," said Grandfather.

"Yes, we may get track of her yet," said Mr. Wentworth, more to comfort his wife than because he really believed it.

Mrs. Wentworth left the work basket, with the needle in the block, just where Abbie had placed it that last afternoon. It seemed to bring her nearer.

## CHAPTER XVII

### THE END OF THE TRAIL

HREE weeks later, along a forest road one afternoon, went eight Indians and three captives. There was a young man of twenty, a woman of thirty-five and a girl of ten or eleven. They had been walking day after day along rough trails in the woods.

Although the captors were savages, ready to kill on the slightest excuse, they were not always wantonly brutal in their treatment of those they carried away.

These three captives were especially fortunate; for, although the hardships of the journey were great and often they could scarcely drag themselves along through the last hour of the day's march, they were not otherwise ill-treated.

There was little opportunity for conversation among them, for the silent Indians were ever on the alert to prevent it; yet the woman and the young man, who seemed to be related, were strongly moved with pity for the girl and had found many ways of relieving the harshness of her lot.

The girl was thin and worn, with scratches on her face and hands, where briers and thorns had caught her as she walked along the trail. Her hair was uncombed and snarled and her clothing torn and ragged. At night, when she lay on the ground or on the bed of boughs sometimes provided, she had often sobbed herself to sleep, thinking of her father and mother, wondering whether she would ever see them again.

For many days they had eaten nothing but parched corn and water, and occasionally some little cakes made by the woman from corn meal carried by the Indians.

On this particular day, as they passed along the more comfortable road, they were allowed to walk together and conversation was not wholly prevented. They could sometimes get glimpses through the trees of a broad river on their left.

Suddenly mustering up the courage to talk, the girl spoke softly to the others, "Where do you think they are taking us?"

"I have no idea," replied the woman. "We seem to be following this great river."

"What will happen to us when we reach the end of our journey?" asked the girl.

"I do not know, child," said the woman. "I

hope nothing worse than what has already happened. I was torn away from my husband and children. He was down in the field, and they were playing at the edge of it, when five of these creatures came and dragged me away. This young man, my nephew, was visiting us. Oh! I shall never see my family again."

Finally, the sun reached the western horizon, and the weary captives hoped they might stop to rest for the night, but the Indians gave no sign of halting their march.

They continued on their way through the dusky forest. Suddenly there was the sound of a cannon. The girl jumped with fright. Were they going to be shot after walking this long distance?

The chilly November evening set in and they drew their clothing more closely around them. The girl was fortunate in having a warm cloak. Finally the road emerged from the woods into a clearing, and a few minutes later their guides halted. Before the captives there loomed the dim outlines of buildings and walls. The Indians began to shout and whoop, bringing more terror to the hearts of those who followed them. Then the voice of a guard was heard calling:

"Who is there?"

"Senecas," was the reply. "Captives."

THE END OF THE TRAIL

A drawbridge was let down. They marched over it and under a stone arch.

They were in Fort Niagara.

They had come along the Portage Road and had entered through the Gate of the Five Nations.

# CHAPTER XVIII

## THE RANSOM

 HILIPPE did not care to go to his room evenings till he was ready to go to sleep. It was too lonely there. This evening he had gone over to the cabin of the gunsmith. The forge sent forth light and heat, making it a cheery place.

"Why do you work so late?" asked Philippe.

"I am going to stop soon. Here is a new gun that is defective. It would be a poor defense in case of attack. I must fix it so it will work right."

"Do you think the English will attack soon?"

"That I cannot say. Our scouts report no sign of it, but we must keep ready all the time."

"I wish my father were alive, he would fight for France and the King."

"Your father was a brave soldier. There was none braver; and yet he was a man of peace, who hated war."

"Yes, I know," said Philippe.

After a moment's silence the smith asked, "Have you his gold-laced coat still?"

"Yes; it hangs in my room always. It is like my father, gay and shining. I like to see it there."

At that moment they heard shouting near the Gate of the Five Nations, and Philippe ran to see what it was about. He was just in time to see the Indians come over the drawbridge and he stood at one side as the line came filing in. He noticed how tired and terror-stricken the captives appeared, especially the girl.

"Why, she is no older than I am," he thought. "What an awful thing to be captured by Indians at that age!"

The group was taken by soldiers of the guard to the Castle. Philippe followed along and stood apart as they filed into the room where the Commandant and his officers were assembled.

It was plain that the captives were wondering what was to happen to them and were looking with eager and anxious eyes at the white men whom they now faced.

"Where did you get these captives?" asked the Commandant.

"Not far from the Mohawk River," replied the leader of the Seneca band.

It seemed to Philippe that he said it proudly, as if he had done a fine deed.

After a little parleying, it was agreed that the Senecas should receive for the young man two blankets and a quantity of bright beads; for the woman, a stroud (a cheap blanket), some ribbons, beads and a brass kettle.

Then came the last of the captives. The Commandant had noticed that she was a pretty girl, with an alert look but badly frightened.

"For the girl we will give two blankets and some mirrors," he said.

The leader shook his head.

"No give her up. She go back to our village."

"Oh, how terrible to be a captive all alone among Indians!" thought Philippe.

The Commandant thought a moment and then said, "We'll give you another blanket."

He turned to one of his aides and said, "Bring those things here, so they can be seen."

The officer went to a room in which goods were stored and soon returned with two men carrying the articles. The eyes of the savages brightened, when they saw the gifts; but the leader remained firm.

"I'll give you money," said the Commandant.

He reached ten livres toward the leader, who for a moment seemed to waver. Then he replied, "No; we take maiden."

"But she is not strong. She cannot do much work."

"She grow. One year, two year, she hoe corn and beans, she grind meal, she scrape skins. She fine maiden. We keep."

He said something to his companions. Two of them stepped up to the girl, one on each side. The others gathered up the blankets, the beads and the kettle that had been given. When the girl saw that she was to go with them, she uttered a deep moan and fell limp in a faint.

"We hungry. Girl hungry. Give us eat," said the leader.

The Commandant ordered food placed on the table for them in the big kitchen. The Indians ate greedily. The woman and the young man ate heartily. No such food had they seen or tasted since they were snatched from home. But, even though she was faint and hungry, the girl could not eat. She sat terrified between two Indians, gazing at the table.

Philippe, standing near the door, could hear the officers back in the other room, conversing.

"We ought to make them give up the girl," said one.

"She is evidently of good family and gently reared. It will be a terrible thing for her," said another.

"What can we do?" said a third. "Can we compel them to release her?"

"How can we?" asked the Commandant. "You know we must not go too far with these savages. If we should take her by force, they would make trouble for us and might take her life before we could save her."

"If we only had something for which they would care very much!" said the first officer.

At this, Philippe stepped into the room and said, "Perhaps I have something they might want. I'll run and fetch it."

He ran across the entrance room, up the little stairway to his room, and took the gold-laced coat from its peg. For a moment he buried his face in it. Then, taking it on his arm, he went down to the Commandant and held it out.

"Offer this," he said.

"Ah, my boy, are you sure you are willing to part with it?" asked the Commandant kindly.

"Yes, to save her," he said.

While this was taking place, the Indians had finished and were rising from the table.

The Commandant held the coat out toward the leader and said, "We give this for the maiden."

He took it in his hands and looked at it with greedy eyes. The gold thread gleamed in the light of the flares. He put it on and strutted proudly about, while the other Indians watched with envy.

"I take coat," he said. "Maiden stay."

The Commandant stepped forward and took the girl by the hand and led her away. He handed her over to two of the officers and then spoke again:

"You will never try to get her away?"

"No; she stay forever. I keep pretty coat—forever."

He led his band out of the Castle toward the Gate of the Five Nations.

When the girl saw them go and realized that she was free, she said earnestly to the Commandant in French, "Oh, I thank you, sir! I do thank you!"

"Here is the one to be thanked," said the Commandant, bringing Philippe forward. "That coat was very precious to him."

She turned to Philippe: "Thank you for saving me! You are good—you are kind!"

She did not realize, till long afterward, all that it meant to him to part with the coat.

The Commandant now inquired of the girl, "How is it you speak French? Are you not English?"

"Yes," she replied, "or Colonial; but I have had a French governess. Can you tell me, sir, where I am?"

"Yes; you are in Fort Niagara. You need have no fear; you will be treated kindly."

To one of the guard, he said, "Take the young man to one of the barracks to sleep. Tomorrow we'll find something for him to do."

To another he said, "The woman and the girl may have that small room upstairs for tonight, till we decide what to do with them." Then he turned to the tired, grateful captives.

"Good night, Madame," he said with a courtly bow, and with a kindly smile for the girl.

# CHAPTER XIX

### THE THREE FRIENDS

HE next morning Philippe over-heard Captain Du Charme say, "The woman brought in captive last night is to be quartered at the hospital, where she will help take care of the sick. My wife will look after the girl."

A little later, Madame Du Charme herself met him in the corridor.

"How is the Mademoiselle today?" asked Philippe.

"She is very tired, Philippe. I am keeping her in bed today. When she is rested and has some proper clothes, I think it would be fine if you would take her around the Fort."

"I'll be glad to," he replied.

"Just think, Philippe, the soles of her shoes were worn clear through, with that long tramp. The shoemaker is making her a new pair. I am making her a dress from a piece of goods in the storeroom. Imagine wearing a lovely silk dress on all that dreadful journey."

Philippe had noticed that these French ladies, wives of some of the officers, were kind to the captives who were brought in.

Madame Du Charme continued, "Mademoiselle must have come from a good home. I like her. She has gracious manners and she speaks French quite well for an English girl."

The second day after that, when Philippe was approaching the Castle, Madame Du Charme appeared with the girl.

"Philippe, this is Abbie Wentworth," she said. "You have seen her before."

Philippe would not have recognized her as the girl with tangled hair and scratched face and a look of terror, who had been brought in captive by the Indians. Her lovely hair was combed becomingly, the scratches on her face had partly healed, her dress of dark blue wool goods looked appropriate for life in a fort, and the frightened look had gone from her face.

"I'm glad to meet you," said Philippe, in French.

"How do you do?" Abbie replied in the same language.

"I have told Abbie you will show her around the Fort," said Madame Du Charme.

They started in the direction of the poplar trees, when Abbie said, "Oh, I thank you again,

Monsieur Philippe, for saving me from the Indians!"

"It was a little thing," he said. "I am only glad I could do it."

"It wasn't a little thing! It was hard for you to part with that coat. Madame Du Charme has told me about it. It was a noble deed and I'll never forget it!"

Philippe, a little abashed by her praise, began to point out various things of interest.

"The big stone building is called the Castle."

"Yes," said Abbie. "It doesn't look the least bit like a fort. It looks more like a great house."

"That is just what it was meant to look like," said Philippe. "The King of France had long wished to have a fort here, but could not get permission from the Seneca Indians. I am afraid the French played a trick on the Indians; for, when they had permission only to build a house, about thirty years ago, they built it like this. You see it looks like a house, but has thick stone walls, like a fort, and has cannon mounted on top."

"It is very gloomy inside," said Abbie.

"Oh, yes, it is dark and gloomy, but it is a comfortable place to live. Did you notice the well in the big front entrance room? In case of siege, we'll have water to drink, you see."

Philippe next took her to the bake-house and

showed her the big ovens, where the bread was baked. Then they went to the gunsmith's cabin and watched the smith repair a cannon.

When they left there, he asked, "How far away is your home?"

"I don't know just how far, but we were three weeks on the way, walking fast every day. It is about forty miles from Albany, in the eastern part of the Province of New York. We are Colonials."

"It must have been terrible, to be seized by those savages and carried off."

"Yes, it was very terrible. I wonder how I lived through it."

"Were they cruel to you?"

"No, not after dragging me away and killing William, our servant, before my eyes. That was horrible. But I was frightened all the time and kept wondering what they would do next. I was cold every night, too, sleeping on the ground. And the food we had was that parched corn. Did you ever taste parched corn, Philippe? It is so hard one can hardly bite it."

"Just once. I didn't like it."

"The worst of it is to be so far from home and not know whether I shall ever see it again. I think of my home day and night. Oh, what shall I do if I cannot go back?"

Philippe wanted to say something comforting,

but what could he say? Finally he said, "You will be treated kindly here, but to get you back home, I don't know whether that could be done very soon."

"Can't I even send a letter to let them know where I am? If I could do that, it wouldn't be so hard."

"I am told it is very difficult. Between this place and your home, there are savage tribes of Indians. If I can learn of a way to send a letter, I'll tell you."

Though Abbie had been taught some French, she found it hard to follow all Philippe said and was often obliged to ask him to repeat his words. Now he remarked, "I wish I knew more English, then sometimes we could talk in your language. I was taught a little of it at a school I attended."

"I'll teach you English," Abbie said eagerly. "Then we can talk in either language."

"Thank you, Mademoiselle," Philippe replied. "And I'll teach you more French."

"What fun that will be!" said Abbie.

At that moment, Philippe saw Red Bird on the far side of the parade ground and beckoned him to come. Red Bird came part way, but when he saw that Philippe was not alone, he stopped.

"Red Bird! Come over here!" called Philippe.

The Indian lad came timidly toward them.

"This is our new friend, Abbie Wentworth," said Philippe.

Abbie said, "How do you do?"

She put out her hand, but Red Bird shrank back. He said something to Philippe which Abbie did not understand.

"Red Bird thinks you would not wish to shake hands with him if you knew it was some of his own tribe that captured you. He is a Seneca. Red Bird wouldn't harm you, though. He is sorry they did it."

"Oh!" said Abbie. Then, in a moment, she added, "Tell Red Bird I would like to be friends with him."

Philippe interpreted this to Red Bird, who nodded.

"Me friend," he said.

"What is it like outside the Fort?" asked Abbie. "It was dark when we came and I couldn't see."

"Let's go up on the wall and I'll show you," said Philippe.

The three of them went to a far corner, where a flight of steps led up to a parapet. As Abbie looked off to the north, she saw a vast expanse of blue water.

"Oh, how beautiful! It looks like the sea," she said. "It can't be the sea, though."

"It is one of the Great Lakes," Philippe replied. "This is Lake Ontario. Have you ever heard of it?"

"Of course, I have seen it on maps at home."

"It is a very large lake. I came in a canoe the whole length of it. Sometimes, when there is a storm, its waves are like the waves of the sea."

"It is beautiful! It is grand!" exclaimed Abbie.

Then she turned toward the west. "That river is the Niagara, I have been told."

"Yes, this Fort stands where the Niagara flows into Lake Ontario."

"Oh, yes, that is plain," said Abbie. "Now I know where I am. This is on the east side of the river, where it flows into the lake."

"You learn quickly," said Philippe.

Red Bird, all this time, was standing by, wishing they could go down to the river, where there was something more interesting to do than looking at the scenery.

"This is a strong fort," said Abbie, as she looked around at the thick walls surrounding the many buildings.

"The English will never take it," declared Philippe.

"Yes, they will. You have no idea how many

English soldiers there are in this country now. The Colonials, too, are enlisting. I have heard my father and the neighbors talk about it."

The soldier on guard came and said, "You must go down now. It is dangerous on the ramparts."

Philippe was looking eagerly off over the lake.

"There comes a fleet of canoes from Montreal," he said, pointing to some boats just rounding into the river. "Let's go down and see them unload."

The three hurried down through the river gate to the dock; but the canoes did not unload. They were on their way up the Portage with provisions for the western forts. After staying an hour, they swept out into the river and turned upstream.

# CHAPTER XX

## THE LETTER

BBIE'S fellow captives, Mrs. Harwood and her nephew, David Brandon, cheerfully did the work assigned them; but Mrs. Harwood continually longed for her home and children.

"I would give anything and go through any hardship, if only I could get back to them," she said.

She and David talked over many plans for making the perilous journey to her home in western Massachusetts.

"If we had a canoe," said he, "I believe we might go down Lake Ontario, and down the St. Lawrence to the neighborhood of Montreal, and then find our way south from there. It would be a long dangerous journey through the woods; but if you want to try it, I'll help."

"I'd do anything," she declared. "I'd take any chance, just to see my children and my husband again."

David went to the Commandant and talked it over.

"I fear you would soon be very sorry," said the Commandant. "In fact I think it would be foolhardy to undertake such a journey, especially at this time of year."

"My aunt's heart is set on it," pleaded David.

"Very well. There will be many dangers; the lake may be rough; in the forests through which you will go, there are hostile Indians. If, however, you decide to take the risk, we will provide the means for you to go."

"We will try it," said David.

Preparations were made at once. The wife of one of the officers gave Mrs. Harwood a warm cloak. Another gave her a wool dress and a cape. She had come there with only the calico dress she had on when she was getting dinner that day in her own kitchen. The officers gave blankets and food, also a gun and ammunition.

"You had better take snowshoes, too, for both of you," said the officer who helped in fitting them out. "The ground may be covered with snow before you reach your homes."

When Abbie heard of their plan, she went to the Commandant and asked permission to go with them.

"No; it would not be safe," he said. "They are grown people and are going on their own responsibility. I feel that I am responsible for you and I cannot permit it."

On leaving the Commandant's room, Abbie said sadly to Philippe, "I am not allowed to go with them."

Philippe saw the look of disappointment on her face, and said, "Perhaps David could take a letter to your home. I'll go and ask him."

In a few minutes he was back with the answer:

"David says he will be glad to take it, and that he will deliver it to your home if he gets through himself."

"Good!" said Abbie, her face brightening. "But I have no paper to write on."

"I'll find some," he replied.

When he came back, he had in his hand a brush and a piece of deerskin.

"There is so little paper for the reports and dispatches that none can be spared," he said, "but you can use these."

She wrote on the piece of deerskin:

Dear Father and Mother:

I am alive and safe at Fort Niagara. I think of you every hour and long to see you. The Indians brought me here, with two others, who are taking this letter to you. The Indians would not give me up till Philippe, an officer's son, gave them a gold-laced coat, which had belonged to his father.

The French officers here and everybody else are very kind to me, but, oh, I do want to come home.

The Commandant thinks it too dangerous for me to
go with Mrs. Harwood and her nephew.
Your loving daughter,
ABBIE.

"I think those folks are unwise to try to go
back," said the gunsmith. "Winter is so near
that they will have a long journey through snow,
after they go as far as they can by canoe."

"Some captives have done it," said Sergeant
La Barre.

"That was in summer; but with winter coming on it will be much harder."

The next day Abbie and Philippe stood on
the river bank below the Fort and watched them
start on their long and perilous journey.

As they left the little dock and reached the
mouth of the river, Mrs. Harwood waved her
hand to those on shore.

In Abbie's heart, as she walked back, there
was a fervent prayer that the two might reach
their homes safely, and that her letter might
come to the hands of her father and mother.

The sending of the letter and watching the
others depart had brought afresh to Abbie her
longing for her own people. She sobbed herself
to sleep that night, wondering how they were
faring at home.

# CHAPTER XXI

### A FINE FRENCH LADY

NE morning, soon after that, the three friends were down at the landing, when a single canoe came in sight up the river. As it glided on, sent along by rapid strokes of the paddle, the words of a song came over the water:

> *"A la claire fontaine*
> *M'en allant promener—"*

"That sounds like Pierre," exclaimed Philippe.

"Who is Pierre?" asked Abbie.

"The voyageur whose keg we found," Philippe replied.

"What keg?" asked Abbie, mystified.

Philippe started to tell her the story, but was interrupted by Red Bird shouting, "Pierre! Pierre!" and waving his hand. The man in the canoe stopped singing and waved his paddle.

"It is Pierre!" exclaimed Philippe. "It is!"

The canoe came quietly up to the little dock and Pierre stepped out.

"Pierre is back, you see," he said, in greeting. "Did I not say I would come back?"

"But it is a long time," said Philippe. "You said you would come back in three weeks."

"I was delayed. I had to make a trip up to Michilimackinac," he explained.

"We found keg," said Red Bird, eagerly.

"The keg? My keg?" asked Pierre in astonishment.

"Yes; came down river," declared Red Bird.

"It could not be!" cried Pierre. "It could never come safe over the Falls and through the whirlpool!"

"It did," insisted Philippe, his eyes fairly dancing.

"It would indeed be a miracle," said Pierre. "Maybe it was some other keg, one that was dropped in the river when canoes were unloading to go up the Portage."

"We never thought of that," said Philippe, fearing lest it turn out to be true.

"Once a baby was dropped in the river there, a baby that was being taken to Detroit."

"Oh, I hope it was rescued," spoke up Abbie.

"Yes, fortunately, it was rescued and taken along," said Pierre.

"Keg has red paint on," said Red Bird.

"Many kegs do," said Pierre. "But we shall see."

Philippe's heart sank at the thought that the keg he had so carefully guarded might contain only raisins or molasses, after all. Then he remembered that Pierre had not met his new friend.

"This is our friend Abbie Wentworth," he said.

"How do you do, Abbie?" said Pierre, taking off his cap and making a grand bow. "How did you happen to come to this far-away Fort?"

"I was brought a captive," she explained.

"Oh, I see," he said. "I am sorry to hear that."

The four of them were walking up the slope to the small gate.

"How is your father, the Captain?" asked Pierre, as they walked along.

"Oh, have you not heard?" said Philippe sadly, his lip quivering. "He was killed on a scouting expedition."

"Your father killed!" exclaimed Pierre. "That is too terrible."

"It true," said Red Bird. "He killed by Mohawk on way to Oswego."

"I am sorry, very sorry," said Pierre kindly. "What a pity it happened so soon after you came across the sea to be with him!"

He placed his hand on Philippe's shoulder and drew the lad to him.

"Pierre will always be your friend," he said.

He and Philippe went up to the room, the others staying down by the door.

"That does look like it," said Pierre, when he saw the keg standing in the corner of the room. "I cannot tell for sure till I open it. This one has been terribly battered about. Let's take it to the gunsmith's cabin. He will have tools for opening it."

He carried it down and the four of them went over to the cabin of the gunsmith, who loaned Pierre a cold chisel, a hammer and other tools. As he worked on it, they stood around and watched breathlessly—Philippe, Abbie, Red Bird and the gunsmith. It took a long time, for the hoops were on tight and strongly fastened.

"It is my keg," said Pierre, after a few minutes. "That is the very hoop I put on and the nail I twisted."

"Good!" said Philippe.

"The doll is probably broken," said Pierre. "It could never stand such knocking about and come through safe."

Red Bird's face clouded. After all their trouble, suppose it were broken! He had not thought of that.

Finally the hoops and the cover were off. Then there were the packings. At last they came to the case in which the doll had taken the journey from Paris across the Atlantic.

The gunsmith and the three children watched, scarcely breathing, as Pierre opened the case.

"She seems all right," he said, in a low voice.
"What a *beau*-ti-ful doll!" exclaimed Abbie.
Pierre turned her all around.
"She looks all right," said Philippe.
"Not a drop of water has touched her and she

is not broken," said Pierre. "Thank Heaven!"

"Good keg!" said Red Bird.

"It is a marvel," said Pierre. "Now the little Marie shall have her doll to play with this winter."

"Where are you going to take her?" asked Abbie.

"To Detroit. I shall start back soon."

"What a stylish doll!" said Abbie.

"She is a fine French lady," said Pierre, holding her up so all could see.

"Now little Marie's father like you again," said Red Bird.

"Yes, he will know that Pierre is not careless. And he shall hear about the lads who risked their lives to rescue the doll. Won't the little Marie's eyes sparkle when she hears that story?"

For two days Pierre stayed at Fort Niagara. Every one in the Fort—the soldiers, the baker, the gunsmith, the officers, the Indians who came to the Fort, the captives who were there—all came to see the lovely doll that had gone over the Falls and had come safely through the whirlpool and rapids.

"I shall not forget what you lads did," said Pierre. "Sometime, it may be, I will take you on a long journey up through the lakes to the farthest end of that great lake—Superior."

The French ladies, the wives of the officers,

made some more clothes for the doll. One made a beautiful cloak from a piece of lovely satin she had brought from France, another made a bonnet, another a dress. When Pierre packed her again in the keg for the rest of the trip, there were many other gifts for the little girl in the far-off fort.

# CHAPTER XXII

## THE LAST BATEAUX

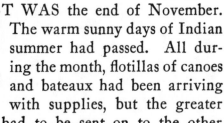T WAS the end of November. The warm sunny days of Indian summer had passed. All during the month, flotillas of canoes and bateaux had been arriving with supplies, but the greater part of them had to be sent on to the other French forts.

In former years, sailing ships had come up the lake with food and other supplies; but this year, since all the ships had been sunk or captured by the English, there was nothing but the canoes and bateaux to bring them. The officers watched anxiously for the coming of the fleets bringing food, in the hope that enough would come to last through the winter.

On one of these November mornings, Philippe and Abbie went to the bake-house to watch the baker. They always liked to see him put the loaves in the oven or take them out.

After the fire that Red Bird had started had burned a long time, the baker would rake the live coals out of the oven and put the loaves in. By taking them on a long-handled shovel, he could place the first ones at the very back of the oven, then cover the whole oven floor with other loaves and shut the door to keep the heat in. What a delicious crust that bread had!

"Is the bread almost done?" asked Philippe.

"Almost," replied the baker. "If you will wait a little while, there may be a nice brown crust for each of you."

As they were waiting, he remarked, "I hope more flour will come before winter. The store-keeper tells me we haven't nearly enough to last till spring."

"Can't you send and get some more if it gives out?" asked Abbie.

"Where would we send?" inquired the baker. "The great forest stretches on and on. There is no city till you come to those over east that belong to the English. Are they going to sell us flour? And if they did, could it be brought here all that distance through a land of hostile Indians? No; all our food, except the game we can hunt, must come from Quebec and Montreal. Soon the lake will be closed up with ice, and then not another boat can come up till next March."

"Does it freeze clear over?" asked Philippe.

"No; it doesn't usually freeze from shore to

shore. But all the bays and harbors are covered with ice, so boats cannot get off from land. Sometimes it does freeze clear across."

"Then what shall we do if enough doesn't come this fall?" asked Philippe in alarm.

"We'll have to go hungry," replied the baker.

"There are many people to feed here at the Fort," said Philippe.

"Four hundred or more," said the baker. "In addition to the soldiers and the captives in the Fort, there are always bands of Indians coming to be fed. Oh, I can tell you it is no easy thing to bake for these hundreds of people, but it would be worse to have no flour at all."

He opened the door of the oven and looked in.

"Done to a turn," he said, as he lifted out the loaves and placed them in rows to cool.

"Here is a bit of fresh brown crust for each of you," he added, slicing it off with a sharp knife.

"Thank you," said Philippe.

"Yes, thank you very much," said Abbie. "Oh, but it tastes good!"

"Let's go and watch for boats," said Philippe. "Perhaps they will come today."

He and Abbie went over to the Lombardy poplar trees, where there was high ground and a good view over the lake. The sun was not shining that day and clouds were scudding before the wind. Whitecaps were on the crests of the waves, making a beautiful sight; but on all that vast expanse of water not a boat of any kind was to be seen.

Philippe tried to climb one of the poplars, so he could see farther, but the branches, growing straight up and hugging the trunk of the tree, made climbing too difficult.

A soldier of the guard came along. "What do you two see out there on the lake?" he asked.

"Nothing but waves," replied Philippe. "We are watching for a flotilla."

"The provisions had better get here soon," said the soldier. "Any day now a cold storm may come and freeze the lake."

"How rough it is getting!" said Abbie.

"The wind is rising every minute," said the soldier. "It is no fun to be on Lake Ontario in one of these November storms."

He passed on. Philippe and Abbie were just starting off to the Castle when they glanced once more over the lake.

"What are those little dark objects on the water up there? Look, Abbie! Could they be boats?" he asked.

"They are not big enough for boats. They might be only wild ducks," said Abbie.

"I think they are boats," said Philippe, "either canoes or bateaux."

Bateaux were larger than canoes, and flatter.

The two stood eagerly watching for a full quarter of an hour. Then Philippe exclaimed, "Bateaux! A lot of bateaux! I am going to tell the baker."

He burst in at the bake-house. "Bateaux!" he shouted. "A flotilla of bateaux."

Then he ran swiftly back to the place where he had left Abbie. The soldier of the guard returned.

"Bateaux!" he said.

"Ten of them," said Philippe.

"What is the matter with your eyes? Or can't you count?" asked the soldier. "Twenty, if there is one."

The boats were going up and down in the troughs of the waves so that it was hard to count them.

"Thirty," said Abbie.

"You are nearer right," admitted Philippe.

Soon the fleet was headed into the river.

"Forty-one," said Philippe.

"Forty-five," said Abbie.

"What's that? Forty-five bateaux? I hope they are all loaded with flour!" It was the baker, who had come up as fast as he could walk, which was not very fast, for he was a stout man.

"Let's go down to the river to see them land," said Philippe.

They found Red Bird there, and the three watched as the bateaux came rounding the little bend and heading in toward the shore.

"It is a wonder that some of you were not capsized," said Sergeant La Barre, waiting at the landing.

"It is one of the worst storms I ever tried to paddle in," said a boatman.

The bateaux were loaded to the gunwales with bundles and bales, sacks and barrels, cases and kegs.

"Are they all for Niagara?" asked one of the officers.

"Yes, they are all to be unloaded here."

Soon a line of men had started up the slope to the small gate, each with a load on his back.

"There's another fleet not far behind us," said one of the boatmen.

"Good!" said Philippe. "Let's go up and watch for it, Abbie."

They ran back to their place by the poplars. It was another hour before they again saw the little dark objects on the surface of the lake. Now they knew at once what they were.

Philippe ran to tell the officer in charge, then came back and tried to see how many.

"Forty!" he exclaimed.

"Fifty!" said Abbie.

As the fleet headed into the river, they could be counted correctly.

"Fifty-one!" said Abbie.

Again they ran to the river to see the fleet come in. Again they watched the unloading and carrying of the goods up the slope to the storehouses in the Fort.

"Now we ought to have enough to eat," said Philippe.

"Yes, it seems good to see all those sacks of flour piled up in the storehouses," said the baker.

"We'll start right back to Montreal in the morning," said the leader of the canoe-men. "With no load we can go fast."

# CHAPTER XXIII

### THE BUILDING OF *The Griffon*

INTER closed in around Fort Niagara. Snow knee-deep covered the ground. Ice formed on the lake for a long distance out from shore. Cold blasts howled around the chimneys of the Castle and the tops of the poplars.

Philippe, Red Bird and Abbie had good times through the day, for one of the carpenters had made them each a sled. The evenings, however, were long and tedious. It was altogether a bleak place, with never a bit of mail and seldom any news from the outside world.

Abbie liked best the evenings when they gathered in one of the rooms of the Castle—the officers, the chaplain, the few French ladies who were there, perhaps a wandering voyageur or a coureur-de-bois. Before the open fire they would sit and tell stories of the great woods or of former days on the Niagara.

One evening in January they were gathered before a big fire of pine logs, which sizzled and crackled cheerily. The officers in their bright uniforms made a brilliant picture in the light of the dancing flames, as the wind whistled and moaned in the chimney.

"What a night!" said Madame Du Charme.

"Why did we come out into this wilderness?" questioned Lieutenant Marchand.

"For the glory of France," said the Commandant. "King Louis has his eye on this great stretch of country in the middle of America."

"We must keep the English from settling in New France," said Captain Du Charme.

"Yes, this country of the Great Lakes and the Mississippi River and the Ohio is ours," declared the Commandant.

Abbie had never heard such claims as these before. She had heard her father and grandfather say that the French were keeping the English from their rightful possessions. It was all very puzzling.

"We must keep the fur trade from falling into the hands of the English," said the Lieutenant.

"If we can only do it!" said the Commandant.

Then Philippe asked a question: "Who came here first, the French or the English?"

"The French," said the Commandant. "Our missionaries and explorers were the first white people on the Niagara. The great La Salle was here several times. He built a small fort where this Fort now stands. Have you not heard how he built the first ship that ever sailed on the Great Lakes above Niagara Falls?"

"Oh, yes, it was called *The Griffon,*" said Philippe.

"Yes, that famous ship was built on the east side of the Niagara, a few miles up the river beyond the Little Fort at the upper end of the Portage."

"Tell us about it," pleaded Philippe.

"You tell it, Father Joseph," said the Commandant.

The Chaplain began: "Just eighty years ago this winter, in 1679, the building of the ship was commenced. All the materials except the timber had to be brought from Fort Frontenac, at the far eastern end of Lake Ontario—the sails, the anchors, the nails, the ropes and many other things. La Salle was bringing them up on a boat along the south shore of Lake Ontario in the month of January. It was a warm winter, not like this one. Desiring to get on faster than the slow-sailing ship could go, he and his chief man, Tonti, left the ship and started on foot to the Niagara River, a distance of about forty miles. He told his men to sail along the shore and bring the boat into the mouth of the river."

"Did they do it?" asked Philippe.

"That is the terribly unfortunate thing about it. Those men let the boat sink with all the supplies on board."

"Let it sink!" exclaimed Philippe. "And did they go down with it?"

"Oh, no, they were all safe. There had come a very warm day, when they went ashore and left the boat anchored near by. They went to sleep and a storm came up, tossed the boat onto a reef and wrecked it. Everything except the lumber for building the ship was on that boat."

"What did he do about it?" asked Abbie, who was now as interested as Philippe. "Did he give it up?"

"Not he," said the Chaplain. "He went up the Portage Hill and then the twelve miles to the spot he had selected for building the ship, near the mouth of a creek, where there would be a good place to launch it; and he set the men to cutting down trees and hewing out timbers for the ship. He had ship-carpenters and a black-smith and other workers. He placed his friend Tonti in charge of the work. You may have heard of the man called 'Tonti of the Iron Hand.' When La Salle had seen the keel laid and the ship well started, he went back on foot for more supplies."

"Did he go all the way back to Fort Frontenac on foot?" asked Philippe.

"Yes, La Salle was not one to be thwarted by difficulties. He went on foot over two hundred miles, back to Fort Frontenac. With two companions and a dog to draw their luggage on a sled, they started on that long journey on snow-shoes in the middle of winter, with only a bag of parched corn for food.

The parched corn gave out two days before they reached Frontenac, and they had nothing to eat while going over the ice at the end of the lake."

"What happened while he was gone?" asked Philippe. "Did the others build the ship?"

"Yes, amid many difficulties, the men worked at the building of the ship. Indians came and tried to hinder it, even threatening the lives of the men. The famous missionary, Father Hennepin, was there and helped in the work and inspired the men by his presence."

"How long was La Salle gone?" asked Philippe.

"He did not come back till August, but he must have sent the supplies on ahead; for when he came back the ship was ready to sail. A great thing it was, to accomplish the building of a ship so far from supplies. With about thirty men he sailed the ship up the Niagara to Lake Erie and on west."

"What did you say was the name of the ship?" asked Abbie, who had not heard the story before.

*"The Griffon,"* said Father Joseph. "Can you imagine the thoughts of the Indians, who had never seen anything larger than a bark canoe, when they saw this large ship sailing before the wind with no paddles to make it go? No wonder they thought it a monster and wanted to destroy it."

"What became of it?" asked Philippe. "Did it make many trips up and down the lakes?"

"That is the sad thing. After all that amount of work and the hardships La Salle went through, the ship sank on its return voyage and was never heard of more. It had a great cargo of furs, too, with which La Salle hoped to make a fortune to pay the expenses of his explorations. It was a terrible blow for him, the sinking of that ship."

"But it didn't discourage him from exploring further, did it?" asked Philippe.

"No; he went on and explored the Mississippi, but of that we haven't time to tell tonight."

"Sometime may we go up where *The Griffon* was built?" asked Philippe.

"I hope you will," said the Chaplain.

It was late. The wind from the lake still shrieked and moaned, as the company dispersed to their rooms.

# CHAPTER XXIV

### THE MAN ON SNOWSHOES

**T**HE month of February was the bleakest one of all at Fort Niagara. Snow lay deep on the ground. Wolves howled in the forest. Sometimes soldiers went into the forest to hunt and came back with a deer, which made a fine change from the salt pork they usually had for meat. Sometimes a group of them, sent to cut firewood in the woods, were chased by hungry wolves and had to run back to the shelter of the Fort.

One morning the world was a glory of shining white. Snowdrifts were piled deep throughout the grounds, snow covered the roofs of the buildings; it covered the walls; the forest trees were white with snow.

That morning, when Red Bird came to the bake-house to light the fire, he came on snowshoes, as he often did.

"I wish I could walk on snowshoes," said Philippe, who had floundered through the deep snow to get to the bake-house.

"I show you," said Red Bird.

After he had lighted the fire, he brought a pair of snowshoes and fastened them on Philippe's feet; but Philippe soon found he could not manage them as well as Red Bird, who had been used to them ever since he was a small boy. When, at the second step, he went headlong into a snowdrift, Red Bird laughed heartily.

Finally, by dint of much trying, he was able before the day was over to take several steps without falling.

"You try every day. You learn after while," said Red Bird encouragingly.

The next day was rainy, and the following night the weather turned cold and froze the falling drops into ice. It covered the trees with a coating of ice that glittered in the sunshine the next morning like myriads of diamonds. Every twig on the trees and bushes seemed made of silver and was sparkling with gems.

Then something happened that surprised them all. Along the Portage Road there came a lone man on snowshoes. The guard on duty above the Gate of the Five Nations saw him and called to him:

"The drawbridge won't work this icy weather. Go around to the small gate."

He came through that gate and went to the

gunsmith's cabin to warm himself. Red Bird saw him and rushed over to the Castle to tell Philippe.

"Pierre! He come!" shouted Red Bird.

"Pierre! Is he here? I thought he was away out west," said Philippe.

"He come. He come on snowshoes," said Red Bird.

The two of them went scampering across the parade ground. They burst in at the cabin with a shout.

"Philippe! *Bon jour, mes garçons!*" cried Pierre. "You two discover me at once."

He was dressed in a suit of deerskin, with a fur cap on his head, fringed leggings that reached above his knees, moccasins on his feet, and his pack on his back.

"Where did you come from? How did you get here in this wintry weather?" demanded the boys.

"I came from Detroit," he replied. "I came on snowshoes over the snow."

"All that three hundred miles?" asked Philippe.

"Why not?" said Pierre. "It is fine weather for walking on snowshoes. The snow is deep and it is packed hard."

Philippe, remembering how difficult it was for him even to take a few steps on the unwieldy things, looked up in admiration at this man who thought nothing of traveling three hundred miles on them.

"But I thought you went trapping in the winter," said Philippe.

"I trapped a while," he replied. "I make up my mind I have a good time this winter. I travel around. I come to see my friends."

He smiled at the boys, who felt a glow of joy that he called them friends.

"Did you get the doll there safe?" asked Philippe.

"Oh, yes, the fine French lady got there all safe and without a drop of water on her lovely clothes. You should have seen the face of the little Marie when she saw it. It was worth all the trouble we took. Her father and mother send their love and thanks to the lads who risked their lives to save it."

"What is that thing on your back?" asked Philippe.

"That is my fiddle. I give you music tonight in the Castle."

So it happened that in the evening a circle of people were gathered around the fire to listen to Pierre as he played his fiddle and sang for them.

"Where did you sleep at night on that long journey?" asked Philippe.

"I find a tree of fir or spruce, with branches coming to the ground. I lie there in the snow under the tree and sleep."

"In the snow?" exclaimed Philippe. "Sleep in the snow?"

"Why not?" said Pierre. "I have a warm blanket of beaver skin. When the big storm came, then it was harder, but I found a cabin some trapper had built. I made a fire and was snug till the storm was over."

"What did you see on the way?" asked Abbie.

"Just snow covering all the ground," he answered. "You should see the snow in the great stretches of country where I traveled. But the most beautiful sight I saw was Niagara Falls. So wonderful! So *magnifique!*"

"Tell us about them," begged Philippe.

"Well, in winter the mist that always rises from the Falls freezes on everything around. This time there was so much ice on the trees and bushes that the limbs bent to the ground with the weight of it. They hung in most lovely curves. Every tiny twig, it is thick with ice like my big finger. When the sun shines they sparkle like diamonds and rubies. Oh, I tell you, it is one grand sight! I would walk all the way from Detroit to see it again."

"I'd like to see it," said Philippe.

"So would I," said Abbie.

Pierre went on: "The rapids—they lash the water into white foam, like beautiful lace on the dress of a queen. It is all so lovely, so superb. I cannot tell it. Then there is a mountain of ice at the foot of the Falls. It must be a hundred feet high. Just below there is a bridge of ice that has formed on the surface of the river near the mountain."

"I wish I could go up there tomorrow," said Philippe.

"You had better not try," said Pierre. "That Portage Hill, it is most slippery and steep. You slip back. You could never climb it on the icy snow."

Abbie was listening breathlessly. What wonderful things were out here in this far-off wilderness!

Pierre sang another song and then the gathering broke up. The next day, when Abbie and Philippe were in the gunsmith's cabin, Pierre came in. He said to her, "This is not so bad a place, here at the Fort, is it?"

"Oh, every one is kind to me," she replied; "but I do wish I could see my father and mother. Sometimes it seems to me that I cannot endure to be away from home any longer."

"That is but natural," he said.

"If only they knew where I am, then they would be comforted," she said.

"We sent a letter by the young man who came along with Abbie, but we don't know whether he was able to deliver it," said Philippe.

"If you would write another letter, perhaps I might take it to your home," said Pierre.

"You?" exclaimed Philippe. "You are not going there, are you?"

"Yes, I have always wanted to go into that eastern country; and now the Commandant wishes me to go and find out some things for him. I start in two or three days."

"But it is dangerous," protested Philippe.

"Not for Pierre," said the voyageur. "Pierre know how to find his way without danger. You should see me when I start."

"What shall I write the letter on?" said Abbie. "I have no paper."

"Me get something," said Red Bird.

He brought her a piece of birch bark. With a quill dipped in ink, she wrote, nearly the same as before:

Dear Father and Mother:

I am at Fort Niagara, safe and well. I was brought here last fall by the Indians who carried me off. I was ransomed by a French boy named Philippe, who gave a gold-laced coat for me, one which he greatly prized. I think of you every hour and am lonely for home. I hope you are all well.

I sent you a letter by David Brandon, who was also a captive and left here in November. I do want to come home.

Your loving Abbie.

At the end of her name, she placed a certain fancy flourish which Mademoiselle Julie had taught her.

"That tells them that I wrote it," she said.

Red Bird rolled up the birch bark and tied it with a leather thong. Two days later Pierre came to get the letter and take leave of the Commandant. His face was painted and he was dressed in the garb of an Indian.

"Will you keep my fiddle for me?" he said to Philippe. "I cannot take it with me."

"Yes," said Philippe; and later he placed it in the corner of his room.

"And now, Mamselle Abbie," said Pierre, "I will tell you something you may be glad to hear, but we French do not like so well. The past year was not good for us; we lost Frontenac and Louisburg in the East, and now we have lost Fort Duquesne."

"Lost Fort Duquesne!" exclaimed Philippe.

"I heard the sad news at Presque Isle. In November a large force of English and Colonials came against the Fort. The small garrison could not defend it, so they burned it and fled. The Colonials were led by a young officer named George Washington."

"Oh, I have heard my father speak of him," said Abbie. "He saved General Braddock's army from destruction."

Pierre placed the letter in his pocket, said good-by to them all, and went out of the Fort on his perilous expedition.

## CHAPTER XXV

### THE SUPPLY SHIP

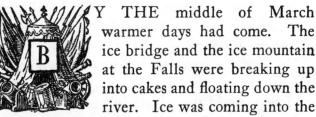Y THE middle of March warmer days had come. The ice bridge and the ice mountain at the Falls were breaking up into cakes and floating down the river. Ice was coming into the Niagara River from the Great Lakes and floating past the Fort. It was exciting to watch the huge cakes bump into each other and swirl around, as they were caught by the currents. Although the ice on Lake Ontario was cracking and floating off toward the St. Lawrence, it was not yet safe for boats to come up the lake.

Food was getting low in the storehouses. So many bands of Indians had come to be fed that the supply had gone quickly.

April came and no new supplies had arrived from Montreal. The time came when the last barrel of pork had been eaten.

One day at dinner, no meat was served, but only a stew of turnips and cabbage.

Philippe and Abbie did not like it much, so

they decided to eat more bread; but they found their ration of bread smaller than before.

"Let's go and ask the baker for some warm bread," said Abbie.

"What can I do for you today?" asked the baker, with a smile, when they came dashing into the bake-house.

"Could we have some bread?" asked Philippe.

"A small piece," said the baker. "We are getting short of flour."

He handed each of them a very little piece of bread.

"I was afraid there wouldn't be enough flour to last through," he said.

"When will more come?" asked Philippe.

"I don't know, son. We are all hoping the ice will go quickly, so the lake will be clear for boats. They say two new ships have been built in place of those destroyed last year by the English. It would be fine if they would come up here with food."

A week later, when Red Bird came to light the fire, the baker said, "You won't have to do this but two or three days more."

"Me no do it good?" asked Red Bird.

"Yes, you do it very well; but no one will have to light the fire, for there won't be any bread to bake. The flour will be gone by that time."

"Oh!" said Red Bird. "What we do then?"

"Go hungry, I s'pose," said the baker.

The next morning was damp, with a chill in the air. The officers were heard consulting anxiously when Philippe went into the big kitchen for breakfast.

"What are we to do if no provisions come soon?" asked Lieutenant Le Maire.

"Cut the rations short. If the men have to go on very short rations, I'll do the same," said the Commandant. "Give each only a quarter of a pound of bread today."

When Philippe and Abbie went to find Red Bird that morning, he was dragging a bag along and had a hammerstone in his hand.

"What is in your bag?" asked Philippe.

"Nuts; walnuts and hickory nuts. Me give for dinner."

"Oh, Red Bird, that is thoughtful," said Abbie.

"We crack 'em," he said.

On a large flat stone they turned the nuts out and began to crack them. Red Bird had his hammerstone. Philippe borrowed two hammers from the blacksmith, one for himself and one for Abbie.

"We must have a big dish to put them in," said Abbie.

She went to the kitchen and asked for a wooden bowl.

"What do you want to do with it?" asked the cook.

"That is a secret," she replied. "I'll bring it back."

The three of them were as busy as beavers for the next hour.

At dinner, when Abbie left the table for a moment and came in bringing the bowl of nuts, there were exclamations of delight around the table.

That afternoon Philippe and Abbie went over to the Lombardy poplars and eagerly scanned the water for boats. The sun had gone under a cloud and the wind was rising.

Red Bird came up and joined them. He had not been there long, when he shouted, "A ship! A ship!"

Philippe and Abbie followed the direction of his finger, as he pointed off toward the horizon.

"Yes, a sailing ship," exclaimed Philippe.

Sergeant La Barre came along. "You are right. It must be one of the new ships, built this winter."

Some soldiers off duty came up to see what the excitement was about.

"A ship! Maybe it has food on board," said Philippe.

"The lake is pretty rough," said the Sergeant.

In an astonishingly short time whitecaps

had appeared and the waves were mounting high. For a while the ship continued to come toward the shore.

"Is she a French ship?" exclaimed Lieutenant Le Maire, who had joined them. "She isn't by any chance an English ship, I hope!"

They stood watching for a few minutes— Philippe, Abbie, Red Bird, the Lieutenant and some soldiers.

"She can't make the mouth of the river," exclaimed Sergeant La Barre. "The wind is too strong against her."

"She is going farther away!" exclaimed Philippe.

Soon it began to rain and the wind blew stronger than ever from the southwest. They all ran for shelter. The storm raged for an hour; and when it was over there was no sign of any ship on the lake.

"Oh, what has become of her?" asked Philippe.

"Maybe she sink," said Red Bird.

He and Philippe went several times to see whether the ship was in sight, but no ship appeared on the lake all that afternoon.

The next morning Lake Ontario was calm again; the ripples sparkled on the great swells in the sunshine of an April day. But it was the middle of the afternoon before Red Bird came running to the Castle, where Philippe and Abbie were playing checkers, with the words "The ship! She come!"

"Let's go down and see it land!" cried Philippe.

They all ran through the little gate down to the landing. Never was there a more welcome sight than that of the new ship, unless it was the sacks of flour and the barrels of pork and kegs of molasses that the men were soon carrying up to the storehouse.

"Where did the ship come from?" asked Philippe of one of the crew.

"It was built at Point au Baril, at the other end of the lake, not far from the place where Fort Frontenac stood," was the reply. "Two ships have been built there by the French this winter and spring. You'll see the other one up here before long."

# CHAPTER XXVI

## WILD FLOWERS AND BEAVER SKINS

 HE middle of April brought two things to the Fort, wild flowers and beaver skins. The wild flowers grew in the woods around it. The beaver skins came in packs down the Portage.

After the coming of spring, not a day passed when Philippe and Abbie did not envy Red Bird his freedom to leave the Fort and wander through the woods. But the Commandant's orders were strict, that they should not go outside except to go down to the landing by the river.

Red Bird took great delight in bringing to them some of the things they could not find for themselves. One day he brought Abbie a bunch of wild flowers picked in the woods.

"Trailing arbutus!" she exclaimed. "Oh, thank you, Red Bird! How lovely they are!"

"Find under dry leaves on ground," he said.

Another time it was a bunch of yellow flowers, yellow as sunshine.

"Adder's-tongues!" she exclaimed. "Oh, Red

Bird, thank you ever so much. They are just like the ones that grew in our woods at home. I wonder whether those are in blossom now."

Later there were hepaticas and bloodroot, violets, spring-beauties and trilliums. He brought Philippe a bird's egg from a nest in the willows, an odd shell washed up on the shore of the lake, an arrow-head picked up from the ground, and, finally, a hammerstone.

One day he came eagerly bringing a head band, with beautiful bead embroidery, which he gave to Abbie.

"Seneca maiden make it," he said.

Abbie placed it around her head.

"It looks fine," said Philippe.

Now that the ice had melted, the Portage again became a busy place. On the rivers and creeks of New France, canoes were being loaded with the winter's catch of furs, and voyageurs were beginning to dip their flashing paddles in the water and come singing down the lakes. Great would be the profit to the French traders and the King if they could keep all this trade.

But in the midst of all these happenings, there was continual talk of an attack by the English.

One morning a band of Indians from the Ohio country, in paint and feathers, came to the Fort. They demanded to see the Chief. When they were taken to the Room of the Commandant, they passed a belt of wampum to him and said, "Our women and children are starving. Give us ten sacks of flour. If the French do not give it, we will go to the English, who will fill our stomachs."

The Commandant gave them a belt of wampum and replied that he could not spare ten sacks of flour but would give four, so that their women and papooses might not go hungry. Pacified, they marched out in single file.

In the afternoon another band came, this time from the region of Detroit. They came with their women and children, who stayed outside while the warriors went into the Room of the Commandant for a council.

"The traders do not give us enough for our furs," said their spokesman. "They give us guns that will not fire and only a few beads and cloth that is not pretty. Our women want bright red cloth for making clothes."

The Commandant replied, "You shall have good guns and many beads and much red cloth. I will order it."

He passed the leader a belt of wampum and the band went out of the Castle.

"See that they are satisfied," said the Commandant to one of his officers. "We can't let them go to the English."

All these things ran together in Abbie's

thoughts, wild flowers and beaver skins, belts of wampum and fear of an attack on the Fort. They made a sort of refrain, as she lay thinking that night before going to sleep; and in the stillness she was aware of two sounds, the roar of the Falls and the singing of frogs in the marshes.

# CHAPTER XXVII

### ABBIE USES HER NEEDLE

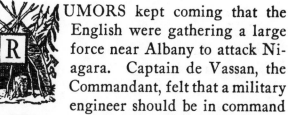 UMORS kept coming that the English were gathering a large force near Albany to attack Niagara. Captain de Vassan, the Commandant, felt that a military engineer should be in command of the Fort in order that it might be strengthened and made ready to resist an attack. The authorities at Montreal appointed, as Commandant, Captain Pouchot, a military engineer.

Near the end of April, two canoes came up the lake, having made the trip very quickly. In one of them was François, Pierre's friend, with whom the boys had come down the Portage the fall before.

"There is a new Commandant coming," he said, "an engineer of the regular French army; and a large quantity of supplies was being loaded for Niagara when we left Montreal. They will be along in a few days."

From the window of his room overlooking the lake, Philippe looked out each morning, to see whether the ships were in sight. Four days later, when he scanned the waters, there they were, two sailing ships, already headed toward the mouth of the river, followed by many bateaux.

He hastened downstairs to tell Abbie and found her in the big kitchen, just finishing her breakfast.

"The two ships are coming!" he exclaimed. "Come on down to the dock."

They hurried to the door, only to meet Red Bird, coming on the run.

"Two ships!" he shouted.

The three hurried down to the landing and saw the two new French ships, built at Point au Baril during the winter, coming into the mouth of the river, followed by more than fifty bateaux.

"Our two ships, with all those bateaux, ought to bring plenty of supplies," said a soldier.

If one ship rounding into the river was a beautiful sight, what was to be said of two ships and the huge flotilla with them? Great was the excitement down by the river, as the fleet came in toward the landing.

"There is Captain Pouchot," said Sergeant La Barre, as he recognized the new Commandant on deck.

"And what a lot of soldiers!" said Abbie.

Soon the men were carrying guns and powder

and cannon balls and other supplies up the slope to the Fort.

Captain de Vassan welcomed his successor, Captain Pouchot, and talked with him about the plans for the repairs. A few days later he departed for Montreal on one of the ships.

Captain Pouchot decided that many things must be done and right quickly. During all the month of May, the soldiers worked like beavers to make the Fort stronger. They made the walls higher; they mounted more cannon on the ramparts.

Soon after the middle of May, scouts came with the report that the English had started for Niagara and were coming up the Mohawk River.

"There are thousands of them," reported a scout. "Many Indians have joined the English forces."

They were still three hundred miles away. Captain Pouchot knew it would take some time for that army, with their food, their artillery, their ammunition, their sheep and oxen, to reach even Fort Oswego. They were coming in canoes and bateaux up the Mohawk River; from that river everything would have to be carried over the big Carrying-place to Wood Creek. Then down the creek, through Oneida Lake, they would go to the Oswego River, which would take them to Fort Oswego on Lake Ontario.

However, they were on the way, and every one in Fort Niagara worked harder than ever to have the Fort ready for the expected attack. The women and girls helped as well as the men and boys. They sewed bags to be filled with earth and used to strengthen the walls and protect the gunners. They made small bags for cartridges.

Thus it was that Abbie, an English Colonial girl, who had been piecing a block in her quiet home when we first saw her, used her needle to sew bags to help in the defense of a French fort.

"It seems an awful thing to have to help against my own people," she said to one of the other captives.

"Yes, but what else can we do? We have been protected and fed here. The least we can do is to help in the defense. Anyway, we have to obey orders."

"I wish there weren't any such thing as war," said Abbie. "I like these French people here. They saved me from the Indians and have been very kind to me. Madame Du Charme has been like a mother to me, and Philippe seems just like a brother. Why do we have to take sides?"

"It is war," said the woman.

"Must we stay here if shooting goes on?" asked Abbie.

"Where else could we go?" replied the woman. "I understand they are making a safe retreat for us under the ramparts, where we'll be out of reach of cannon balls."

Great flocks of wild geese were flying north these days and the woods were full of the songs of birds; but there was anxiety in the hearts of the people at the Fort.

However, when Philippe saw the piles of cannon balls, the vast quantities of powder taken into the powder magazines, and the cannon mounted on the walls, he said to the gunsmith, "The English can never take this Fort."

"We must not be too sure," said the gunsmith. "The scouts report that many Colonials are joining the English forces. Many of the Indians who promised to be on our side have gone over to the English. We cannot quickly get reinforcements, either from the French forts to the west or from Montreal."

"Then do you think that the Fort will be captured by the English?" asked Philippe.

"We cannot tell. The best we can do is to keep close watch that they do not come upon us unawares."

# CHAPTER XXVIII

## THE ENGLISH

LL through June the scouts sent out by Captain Pouchot kept reporting that the English had not come to Oswego. The first of July came and still the Indian scouts reported that the English were not there. Captain Pouchot expected that they would encamp there for a few weeks when they did come, giving him time to send for reinforcements.

It was a hot place in the Fort these July days. Abbie and Philippe liked to go to one of the few cool places, under the poplar trees, and play quiet games by the hour.

On the afternoon of July 6th, as they were playing mumblety-peg, Red Bird brought Abbie a water lily, picked in the creek at the Little Marsh, where he and Philippe had gone on an October day the fall before.

"Oh, how lovely!" said Abbie. "I do like water lilies. At my home I used to gather them in the pond down near our woods."

"Bring big heap tomorrow," Red Bird promised.

"Thank you, Red Bird," said Abbie.

"Me bring turtle for Philippe, if catch him," said Red Bird with a grin.

"You'll not be able to catch one," said Philippe. "Don't you remember how they would slip off the log just before we touched them?"

"Turtle, he quick," said Red Bird. "Get him some day."

While they sat there talking, a scouting ship which Captain Pouchot had sent down the lake, came back into the river. The men on it reported that there were no English at Fort Oswego.

Early the next morning, Red Bird slipped out and started for Abbie's water lilies. It was a long walk, four miles, but in the cool of the morning and in the shade of the forest, he did not mind it. In an astonishingly short time, however, he was back at the Fort, with no water lilies in his hands. He ran to the Castle. The guard at the door stopped him.

"Want to see Captain Pouchot," said Red Bird.

"Oh, you can't see the Commandant," said the guard. "No one can see him now except on important business."

"Much important," insisted Red Bird. "Big news."

"News?" asked the guard. "What news?"

"Tell Captain Pouchot. Me scout."

Just then Philippe appeared. Red Bird whispered to him.

"He *has* important news. The Commandant will want to hear it," said Philippe, greatly excited.

Red Bird was allowed to go to the Room of the Commandant.

"What is your news?" asked Captain Pouchot.

"The English! They come!" said Red Bird.

"The English? Where are they?" asked Captain Pouchot in astonishment.

"The Little Marsh," replied Red Bird. "Many soldiers! Many boats!"

"Can it be possible?" said the Captain. "Only yesterday, at four o'clock in the afternoon, the ship reported that no English were to be seen at Oswego."

"It true," Red Bird asserted stoutly. "Send scout to see."

At that moment one of the guard came in and saluted.

"Seven English barques are cruising under the bank of the lake," he said.

"English barques? On the lake here?" asked the Commandant.

"Yes, sir."

"You must be right, Red Bird," said the Commandant. "You were the first to report the English army."

He quickly issued orders: "Send a scout down the lake toward the Little Marsh! Man the bastions! Fire on the English barques!"

At the firing of the cannon, the barques took to the open lake.

Soon a scout came in and reported that a great many soldiers were on land, around the Little Marsh, with camp fires burning.

An hour later an Indian scout reported that he had seen Sir William Johnson standing before a tent in the English camp, with some of his officers and an Indian Chief.

There was forest all the four miles between the Fort and the marsh, and there was a bend in the shore of the lake, so nothing could be seen from the Fort. A bateau, immediately sent down the lake toward the east, reported fifteen or twenty barges, each with about twenty soldiers on board, entering the mouth of the Four-Mile Creek, at the Little Marsh.

Thus unexpectedly did the English come and surprise the garrison at Fort Niagara. They had been four days coming along the south shore of Lake Ontario from Oswego, in hundreds of open boats, camping on shore at night. There they were, only four miles away, about two thousand two hundred English and Colonial soldiers under General Prideaux and about nine hundred Indians under Sir William Johnson.

In the Fort were about five hundred soldiers, about forty workers and a number of captives, several of them children.

At once a runner started up the Portage Road to carry the news to the other French forts and ask for reinforcements. He was to tell Sieur Chabert at Fort Little Niagara, and then go on to Presque Isle, Le Boeuf and Venango.

The next morning, a soldier with a white flag appeared in the clearing. He brought a letter from General Prideaux, saying, "The King of England, having given me the government of Fort Niagara, has sent me thither to compel its surrender, if necessary by superior forces."

Captain Pouchot replied, "The King of France has intrusted me with this place and I find myself in condition to defend it."

Thus did the siege of Fort Niagara begin, July 7, 1759.

# CHAPTER XXIX

### THE SIEGE

T ONCE there was great activity in the Fort. Although four miles of forest still separated the French from the English, gunners manned the cannon on the ramparts and also on the roof of the Castle, ready to defend the Fort.

At Fort Little Niagara, the Commandant, Chabert, carried all the provisions, the horses, the cattle and the merchandise across the wide river to the Canadian side, where he thought they would be safe. Then he set fire to the Fort. Everything made of wood burned to the ground, leaving the Big Stone Chimney standing. That was the end of Fort Little Niagara. He then came down the Portage, with the seventy others from the Little Fort, and succeeded in reaching Fort Niagara.

On July 10th, Captain Pouchot sent other runners to the western forts, lest the one already sent should not get through. He again urged the officers to hasten to his relief with reinforcements. Each night the English advanced their cannon and intrenchments nearer, and their cannon balls and bombs began to fall into the Fort. Both the French and the English sometimes fired red-hot shot.

Casks of water were placed near the wooden buildings, with buckets near by, so that, when red-hot balls set them on fire, it could quickly be put out. Carpenters were stationed there to cut away burning wood.

During the early part of July, boats could go in and out of the river, but the entrance was finally closed, with one French ship still out on the lake. This is how it happened. On the morning of July 17th, when the fog cleared away, it was discovered that the English had placed several cannon across the river during the night and were firing into the Fort from the western side. A cannon ball that day came down one of the chimneys of the Castle and rolled under the Commandant's bed.

No French boat was supposed to enter the river from the lake. One did, however, a few days later. It slipped by in the dead of night, a canoe, in which there was only one man.

Early the next morning, when Philippe went out to see how things were going, he almost ran into that man.

"Oh, Pierre! When did you come?" he asked.

"In the night," was the answer. "I slipped by the English guns."

"We were afraid something had happened to you," said Philippe.

"Many things happened to me. I was taken prisoner by the English, but I escaped. I am just up from Montreal."

"Abbie will want to see you," said Philippe.

"I want to see her," said Pierre; "I have news."

"I will find her for you," said Philippe. "I have your fiddle yet. I have kept it all safe."

"Thank you," said Pierre. "Will you keep it a while longer? Pierre has no place for his fiddle now, but I take it sometime."

They found Abbie in the Castle, sewing bags.

"Oh, Pierre, Pierre," she said, "I am so glad you are back safe."

"I am most happy to be here and to report that I delivered your letter," he said. "I found the house without difficulty, a month after I left here. I tied the letter to the door-latch and knocked loudly on the door."

"Did you see my father and mother?" asked Abbie eagerly. "And are they well?"

"That I do not know, but I know they received the letter, for I watched from the shelter of an evergreen while a gentleman opened the door and found it."

"How can I ever thank you enough?" exclaimed Abbie.

"It was nothing," said Pierre. "I was most glad to do it."

"And then he was taken prisoner," said Philippe.

"But surely not there," said Abbie.

"Oh, no; that was afterward. I was rash. I went into the very camp of the English, as they were getting their forces together. I was discovered and made a prisoner. I escaped, but not in time to reach here before they did."

"I am so glad you have come," said Philippe. "Do you think the Fort will have to surrender?"

"I fear it will unless help comes quickly. Captain Pouchot has asked me to be ready to go on a moment's notice with an important message."

"Then we may not see you again?" said Abbie.

"You may not," he replied. "But if the Fort is captured, Philippe, and you have nowhere to go, remember that Pierre will always be your friend. I like to take you with me on my voyages and teach you to be a voyageur; then you would always be going up and down the rivers and the lakes. Wouldn't you like that?"

"How could I find you?" asked Philippe.

"Well, Detroit will still be left. If you could make your way there, some one would always

know how to find Pierre. I must now return to
the Commandant. Adieu, my good friends."

Each day the garrison looked for the reinforcements, but they did not come. Each day
the English came nearer and their artillery did
more damage.

The soldiers in the Fort did not go to bed,

but slept in their clothes, wherever they chanced to be.

"What shall we use for more bags?" asked one of the women when the cloth was all gone.

"Take the mattresses from the officers' beds," was the order.

Later there came a time when there was no material for cannon wads.

"Take the straw that came out of the mattresses," was the order.

When that was gone, they took the sheets from the beds for cannon wads.

During the siege a great misfortune came to the English, when their commander, General Prideaux, was killed by the explosion of one of their own guns. Sir William Johnson, who had been leading the Indians, took command of the whole English army; and the siege went on.

Red Bird was here, there and everywhere in the Fort. He and Philippe helped put out many a fire, when red-hot cannon balls dropped on the roofs of the wooden buildings. Sometimes they caught a glimpse of the baker; sometimes they caught a glimpse of the gunsmith, working fast to repair the guns.

One day Philippe was in the gunsmith's cabin, watching him work.

"It would be well if King Louis had sent more guns," said the smith. "Every day many of them are ruined. They are so badly broken that we cannot make them fit to use any longer."

"What shall we do when they are all broken?" asked Philippe.

"We'll have to stop fighting then. The English will take the Fort."

"Oh, do you think that will happen?"

"It may. When these are gone, that is the end; for we can't get any more."

Two soldiers, off duty, came into the cabin.

"How does the fighting go?" asked the gunsmith.

"Bad; the English are getting closer all the time," said one of them.

"For my part, I don't care much," said the other. "I'll fight as long as there is a chance of keeping the English out of the Fort, but America is no place for us to bring our wives and children. Ugh! A wilderness! Nothing but forests and wild animals and Indians!"

"You are right," said the first. "I'd like to see Paris again and the lovely villages of my France."

"Many of us will never see it again," said the other. "Every day some poor fellows are hit and breathe their last."

"If the reinforcements do not arrive soon, we might as well give up," said the first soldier.

"How can five hundred of us keep off three thousand of the English?"

"We have plenty of powder and shot," said the other. "There is still a vast deal of powder."

"Powder is of no use without guns that will work," said the smith. "Seven of us have been busy almost day and night, trying to keep the muskets in order; but look at that pile of guns in the corner. They are beyond repair."

# CHAPTER XXX

### HOPES AND PLANS

N THE lake, English ships patrolled back and forth. No more could fleets of canoes come sweeping into the river from Montreal. No more did canoes come down the river loaded with furs. Pierre was absent, but no one knew where.

During the firing of cannon the next morning, Philippe and Abbie sat in the Castle, talking.

Philippe had been so successful in learning English, that now they often used that language, as they were doing on this occasion.

"Will this siege never end, Philippe?" Abbie asked. "Must we live in danger much longer?"

"I think it won't go on much longer. Every day some of the ramparts are broken down."

"Why don't those reinforcements come?"

"Who knows? They may be on the way."

Just then a cannon ball struck the Castle and shook it to its foundations.

"Oh!" cried Abbie. "What shall we do?"

"This building is safe," said Philippe. "It has thick walls. Not a shot has gone through them yet."

"But one may. Where can we go to be safe?"

"This building is as safe as any place in the Fort. The wooden buildings may catch fire, but this will not."

After a few minutes the firing ceased and they went on talking.

"Philippe, what will you do if the French have to give up the Fort? Will you go back to France?"

"I don't want to. You see, Abbie, I have no home there now. I have no near relatives to whom I could return."

"Oh! How unfortunate to have no home!"

"I suppose I'd have to go to Montreal, but I don't know any one there, either. I could go with Pierre, and he would teach me to be a voyageur. I like Pierre; but ever since I can remember, my father has said he desired me to be educated and have some profession. It was my mother's wish, too. If he had lived and we had returned to France, that is what I would have done."

More than ever, Abbie saw what the gold-laced coat had meant.

Suddenly she burst out with, "Why does there have to be war? It has killed your splendid father and left you without a home. It has killed many soldiers in the Fort. Why couldn't these questions be settled without fighting?"

"I have often thought of that," said Philippe. "It would surely be a better way."

They were silent for a few moments, while the cannon balls whizzed through the air outside.

Philippe spoke again: "Whatever happens, Abbie, and wherever I go, I shall never forget the good times we have had here together."

"Nor I, Philippe."

Red Bird came rushing in. "Come, Philippe! Gunsmith's cabin on fire!" he shouted.

The two boys ran to throw water on the burning roof. Abbie went back to sewing bags.

On July 23rd an Indian carrying a white flag appeared in the Portage Road. Captain Pouchot answered by showing a white flag, and four Indians came down the road and entered the Fort. They bore letters from the officers of the reinforcements, saying that they had received Captain Pouchot's letters and were on their way.

"We have six hundred French and a thousand Indians," the letters said.

This message brought joy to all in the Fort. Surely, with that help, they could fight off the English and compel them to end the siege.

Captain Pouchot wrote a letter in reply, containing advice about reaching the Fort, and gave a copy of it to each of the four Indians to carry back.

That day the walls became so broken down in places that packets of beaver skins from the storehouses were piled up about the cannon to give some protection to the gunners. Blankets and shirts from the storehouses were used for cannon wads.

# CHAPTER XXXI

### THE BATTLE

N THE meantime, Pierre had gone up the west side of the river, taking a message to the coming reinforcements. Leaving the Fort by night, he had paddled his canoe up the river as far as he could and had then gone on foot around the Horseshoe Falls. He had been told that he would find a canoe hidden in the bushes on the river bank above the Falls. He pushed it into the water and paddled up the river toward the place where the city of Buffalo now stands.

About mid-day of July 23rd, when he had almost reached Lake Erie, a strange and wonderful sight met his eyes. He beheld hundreds of canoes entering the Niagara River from the lake, each one full of men. There were soldiers in brilliant uniforms, voyageurs in buckskins, traders and coureurs-de-bois, young men of the French nobility in their gay clothes, Indians from many tribes, in war paint and feathers.

"The reinforcements!" exclaimed Pierre. "The soldiers from the western forts!"

He paddled swiftly toward the head of the huge fleet and found the canoe carrying the leading officers.

"A dispatch from Captain Pouchot," he said, as he handed the letter to one of them.

He then dropped back and joined the great fleet of nine hundred canoes, which went sweeping down the river. They stayed that night on an island in the river. Early the next morning they paddled over to the place where the Little Fort had stood.

Many were the exclamations of surprise when they saw Fort Little Niagara in ruins, burned to the ground. Most of the Frenchmen had passed it on their way to the west.

"The Big Stone Chimney still stands, though," said one of the soldiers.

"How many times have I warmed myself at the fireplace in that chimney!" said another.

They marched down the Portage Road, the last of the French forces to go down the famous Carrying-place. On down the Portage Hill went this great throng toward the Fort, seven miles north.

Sir William Johnson had been informed by his scouts of the coming of the reinforcements and had sent a large force of soldiers and Indians to meet them and give battle.

On that morning, the 24th of July, it was cloudy with frequent showers. Captain Pouchot did not know of the arrival of this army till he heard heavy firing, a mile away, in the woods up the road. He went to the bastion above the Gate of the Five Nations to watch; there he stood and listened.

He could not see what was going on, because of the rain and because of the woods that shut off his view. He hoped it was only a skirmish in which the French forces would come out ahead; but it was the battle that was to decide the fate of Fort Niagara and of New France.

Captain Pouchot and the garrison in the Fort hoped in vain. About two o'clock that afternoon an Indian came to the Fort and told him the bad news.

"The reinforcements have been defeated," he said. "The officers were all made prisoners. All the soldiers that were not killed or captured have been chased back through the woods."

"It can't be possible!" declared Captain Pouchot.

But it was true. That great body of men who had gathered from the western forts and had so gaily come down in the nine hundred canoes had been surprised and defeated in a battle about a mile up the road, at a place called La Belle Famille.

Two hours later the beating of a drum in the English camp was heard, a signal for a truce. An English officer was sent to the Fort to tell Captain Pouchot that it was indeed all true.

Still he could not believe it. He asked that some of his own staff might go to see whether it was so. They went to the English camp and found all the surviving officers of the army of reinforcements in a tent, prisoners.

Then Captain Pouchot called his officers together for a council. When they found that the walls of the Fort had been broken down in many places, that there were only one hundred and forty muskets left, that the soldiers were so tired that they fell asleep while trying to fire their guns, and that there was nothing left for cannon wads, they decided to surrender.

# CHAPTER XXXII

### REUNION

LL that night the officers of the two armies were engaged in making the arrangements for turning over the Fort to the English. They signed Articles of Capitulation by which it was agreed that the French soldiers, including the workers, like the baker and the gunsmiths, should be allowed to march out of the Fort without being harmed by the Indians; that, being prisoners of war, they should embark on bateaux and be taken to Fort Oswego and thence to New York, to be sent to England. It was agreed that the French women and children and the Chaplain should be sent to the nearest French post, which was Montreal.

At seven o'clock the next morning, July 25th, 1759, the English army marched in and took possession of Fort Niagara, under their General, Sir William Johnson.

With a heavy heart Philippe saw the Lilies

of France come down and the Crosses of Great Britain go up.

Soon he noticed that the French officers were gathering together their personal belongings and taking them to the powder house.

"Bring your chest," said one of them. "We'll put it there with the rest."

Philippe closed it and handed it to the officer, who hastened away. Then the boy's eyes lighted on Pierre's fiddle, standing in the corner of the room. He seized it and hurried after the officer, but was ordered back by one of the guards.

He stood outside the Castle, where Red Bird soon came. All was confusion around them.

"I wish I could find a place to hide this fiddle," said Philippe. "I promised to keep it safe for Pierre."

Red Bird's face lighted up. "Me know good place," he said. "Bring fiddle."

They hastened away and came back a few minutes later, empty handed.

"Fiddle safe," Red Bird was saying.

"No one will find that place," said Philippe.

It was understood that the Indians should not enter the Fort while the French remained, but in spite of the efforts of the guards, about five hundred of them scaled the walls and swarmed over the grounds.

The French soldiers, with their officers, were

drawn up on the parade ground in line of battle, each with his gun in his hand and his haversack between his feet, ready to march down to the boats. There they stood, all that hot day, waiting.

"Why don't we start?" was the question often asked impatiently.

"There is a storm on the lake," was the reply. "The waves are so high that the bateaux cannot venture out."

Meanwhile the order was issued, "Place all the French women and children in the gunsmith's cabin, under guard, to protect them from harm."

Another order was, "Place all the captives in the big chapel, under guard, for protection."

Abbie and Philippe were in the big entrance room of the Castle, wondering what was to happen next, when two English officers came in.

"You are to go to the gunsmith's cabin with me," said one of them to Philippe.

"Must I go to Montreal?" Philippe asked.

"It is the order," was the reply.

"And you are to go to the chapel with the rest of the captives," said the other officer to Abbie. "You need not be afraid. You will be protected there."

"Good-by, Philippe," said Abbie, a little tearfully, as she turned to go.

"Good-by, Abbie," he replied, as he went with the officer.

A few hours later, Indians swarmed into the Castle and pillaged it of everything they could find. One of them came out with a girl's tattered pink silk dress and went through the parade ground, holding it aloft.

Finally, the next afternoon, after thirty hours, the order was given to march down to the landing. Those in the gunsmith's cabin, the French women and children, marched through the small gate to the river and boarded a bateau.

The line of soldiers began to march, guns and baggage in their hands, drums beating. They marched down to the landing. Bateau after bateau came up to the landing, was quickly filled with soldiers and pushed away, each man giving up his gun as he stepped aboard.

When about half of them had left the Fort, there came rushing into it an English officer. He saw the line of soldiers waiting to go through the gate and said to one of them, "Is there a girl named Abbie Wentworth here in the Fort?"

The soldier did not understand English and shook his head. The Englishman then went to one of the officers and put the same question.

"Yes, there has been; she must be here somewhere," was the answer.

"Where is she? Oh, where is she? I must find her at once!"

"I don't know," was the reply. "No one knows where any one is."

Finally the English officer came to the baker, who was standing in line, ready to march.

"Do you know where a captive girl named Abbie is?" he asked.

"Abbie, the lovely mamselle?"

"Yes; where is she?"

"I'll find out," said the baker.

He spoke to the officer nearest him; "Where is Abbie, the captive girl?"

"She is probably with the other captives, wherever that is," was the reply.

The baker, looking perplexed, stood thinking what to do next, when Red Bird came along.

"Oh, Red Bird, do you know where Abbie is?" he asked.

"Me find," said Red Bird.

"Come and tell this English officer when you find out," said the baker. "I must march now."

In a few minutes Red Bird came running back.

"Come," he said.

They went to the door of the chapel, where English soldiers were on guard.

"Is there a girl here named Abbie Wentworth?" asked the officer.

The guard called, "Abbie Wentworth is wanted."

In a moment she came to the door.

"Abbie! Abbie!" called the English officer.

"Oh, Father!" she cried. "Father!"

She sprang to his arms and buried her face on his shoulder and wept for joy.

"There, there, Abbie, don't cry now. Thank God I have found you. And thank God you are safe."

"How do you happen to be here?" she asked, as soon as she could speak.

"When I got your letter, I enlisted in the

English army, hoping I could find you in that way. They were already gathering to come here. I came with them to Fort Oswego, but when they started on I was very ill and was left behind."

"And you came on alone?" she asked.

"Two days ago, I was well enough to start. I came in a canoe with an Indian to paddle it. We have been coming day and night."

"Oh, Father, it was terrible to be seized and carried off," she said, as she clung to him.

"There, don't think of it any more. You are safe now. I am going to take you home."

"Is Mother well?" she asked. "How are Charles and Sally? And Grandmother and Grandfather? How is Lydia?"

"They are all well but Grandfather," was the reply. "He died during the winter. It has been a very lonely and anxious house without you."

Just then there came to the door another man, who seemed to be looking for some one. Abbie looked up just as he was saying to the guard, "I wonder where the French boy Philippe is and the girl named Abbie. Do you know?"

The guard did not understand and was about to order the man away, when Abbie ran to the door.

"Please let him in," she begged.

"Let me have your gun and knife," said the guard. The man gave them up and entered.

"Pierre!" said Abbie. "Oh, Pierre, then you were not killed in the battle?"

"No; only wounded a very little. Pierre is quite alive," he said. "I come back to see if I can help you and Philippe."

"Father, this is the man who took the letter to you," she said.

Captain Wentworth shook hands with the voyageur. "I am most grateful to you, sir, most grateful."

Abbie interpreted it.

"It was nothing," said Pierre. "Who wouldn't go to the same trouble for the mamselle Abbie?"

"It was a great deed," said Captain Wentworth. "I'll find some way to reward you."

Suddenly he asked, "Where is the boy who saved you from the Indians? Is he here now?"

"Philippe? I do not know where Philippe is," Abbie replied. "We were separated and I was sent here."

Red Bird was standing just outside the door and heard the name.

"Philippe, he gone in bateau. Gone to Montreal."

"Oh, Father, Philippe did not want to go to Montreal. Couldn't we take him home with us? He has no home now."

"Philippe, who saved you, has no home?"

said Captain Wentworth. "Of course we would take him with us if he were here."

"How can we find him? How can we get him?" asked Abbie in excitement.

"I'll go in a canoe. Maybe I'll overtake him," said Pierre.

"Oh, could you?" she asked eagerly.

"I'll try," he promised.

"I'll first have to get an order from the General," said Captain Wentworth.

He found the General busy with many things; but when Captain Wentworth explained that this French boy had saved the daughter of a Colonial gentleman from captivity, he wrote this order:

> The boy, Philippe de Croix, is to be allowed to leave the bateau and return with the bearer.
>
> WILLIAM JOHNSON.

Captain Wentworth rushed back to the chapel and gave the order to Pierre, who hastened away.

While they were waiting, Abbie and her father talked of many things.

"Did you ever receive the letter I sent you by David Brandon?" asked Abbie.

"Yes; just before I left home, he brought it."

"Then David got back safe. Did his aunt, also?"

"Yes, he said they went through terrible hardships, but reached their homes alive and well."

"I wanted to go with them," said Abbie, "but the Commandant would not allow me."

"I am very thankful that he did not allow you to go," replied Captain Wentworth.

# CHAPTER XXXIII

## PHILIPPE'S REWARD

IERRE ran down to the dock. The surface of the water in the little cove was covered with bateaux, which were being drawn up to the dock one after another. Into each bateau fifteen or twenty French soldiers would enter, with English soldiers for guard, besides the canoe-men to paddle.

Pierre looked eagerly around for a canoe. The first one he tried to take, he was ordered by an officer to leave alone. Then he spied another one, which did not seem to be in use. Again he was ordered to leave it alone.

Strange, if after going to all the trouble of getting the order for Philippe, he could find no canoe with which to go after him! The third time, he pulled out the order and showed it.

"But that is an order for a boy, not a canoe," said the officer.

"The boy is on the lake. Can I get him without a canoe?" asked Pierre. "The General's order is to get the boy."

"Take that canoe," said the officer.

Pierre jumped in and made his way between bateaux to the open water. Already many had gone out of the river, and a few were nearly out of sight.

Pierre's paddle began to fly with swift strokes. He passed first one bateau and then another, going in his light canoe faster than the heavily-laden bateaux could go.

Now that the storm was over, the lake was covered with great waves that rolled lazily toward the shore and lifted the canoe high on their crests. The ripples gleamed under the afternoon sun.

Pierre had to find out in which of the bateaux Philippe was. He glanced at each one he passed, but to his disappointment found them full of men. In the bateau for which he was searching, there would be women and children.

He hailed some of them: "Do you know which bateau is going to Montreal?"

No one knew. Finally, after passing many boats carrying French officers and soldiers, he noticed a bateau some distance in advance of all the rest.

He redoubled his efforts, each stroke of the paddle sending the canoe far ahead.

"What if that is not the one?" he was thinking, as he came near.

Ah, yes, there was a boy in it. He paddled faster and called to the officer in charge:

"Hold! An order!"

He waved it toward the boat. The boatmen stopped paddling and slowed the bateau.

Philippe recognized the man in the canoe and waved his hand to him.

Pierre came alongside and handed up the order, which the officer read aloud:

"The boy, Philippe de Croix, is to be allowed to leave the bateau and return with the bearer."

"Which is Philippe de Croix?" he asked.

Philippe rose in his place.

"Do you wish to return with this man?" the officer inquired.

"I do, sir," answered the boy.

"Very well, then."

Philippe wondered why Pierre was so anxious to take him back; but, with hurried farewells to those he was leaving, he climbed over the side into the canoe.

"Let me have the order back," said Pierre. "I may need it to get into the Fort."

It was passed back and the bateau went on. Pierre turned about and started back to the Fort.

"When did you come?" asked Philippe. "I feared I would not see you again."

Pierre told him how he had met the reinforcements and had come back with them. He told how he had been lucky enough to escape when the battle was over and had hidden till the next day and come back to the Fort.

"I came to see if I could help you and Abbie," he said.

"Why am I to go back?" asked Philippe. "What is to happen to me?"

"Ah, that I must not tell," said Pierre. "We will let a friend of yours tell that."

How different was this canoe trip from that one the fall before, when he had first come to Fort Niagara! The forest-clad shores looked just as they had looked on that day. The great blue lake, stretching off to the horizon, looked the same. Everything else, how different! Then, he could look forward to meeting his father. Now, what was before him? Why did the General send for him?

They came into the mouth of the river, meeting many bateaux full of French soldiers on the way out, and landed at the little dock.

Pierre stepped out, Philippe after him, and they hurried up to the small gate.

"We are to go to the chapel," said Pierre.

The last of the line of French soldiers had marched out. Everywhere were signs of the damage done by the enemy's cannon.

← 218 ⫸

When they entered the chapel, Pierre announced proudly, "I found him."

Abbie and her father, Pierre and Red Bird stood there together.

Philippe saw with astonishment the tall English officer and wondered what had happened in his absence. Before he had time to ask what was wanted of him, Abbie spoke:

"Oh, Philippe, I am so glad you have come back! This is my father. He's just come!"

Philippe's surprise was only increased by this announcement, but he managed to say, "How do you do, Monsieur Wentworth?"

"I am glad we overtook you, Philippe," said Captain Wentworth. "We would like you to go with us to our home."

"Oh, that would be most wonderful," said Philippe. "You mean for a visit?"

"Oh, no, not just a visit," said Abbie. "We want you to live there."

"That was a splendid thing you did for my daughter," said Captain Wentworth. "I would like to repay you, as far as one can pay for such a fine deed."

"It was little," said Philippe.

"It saved her from a terrible life; it saved us from a great sorrow," said Captain Wentworth. "Will you go with us and be as a son in our household? I will give you whatever education you may wish."

"There is nothing in all the world I would like better," said Philippe.

"It is agreed, then," said Captain Wentworth. "We will go back tomorrow, with some of the other officers, and join the army going on to Albany."

Red Bird had stood near by, not understanding much of what was said, but guessing most of it.

"Pierre, we hope you will come to see us sometime," said Abbie. "You know the way."

"I come on snowshoes, in the winter," said Pierre. "I am so happy that matters have turned out so well for my young friends. You will not forget Pierre, will you?"

"Forget Pierre? Never!" she declared. "Sometime we will hear the knocker on our front door and when we open it, there Pierre will be standing."

"And maybe Red Bird will be with me," said Pierre.

"I hope he will," said Captain Wentworth. "You will both be welcome, always."

"Me tell my tribe. Your house always safe now," said Red Bird.

# CHAPTER XXXIV

## A NEW DAY

WHILE the older ones were talking, Philippe drew Red Bird aside and said, "We've had good times together here, Red Bird. I'll never forget you."

"Me never forget," said Red Bird. "Me hope stars shine bright for you always."

"Thank you," said Philippe. "And where will you go?"

"Back to my tribe. Some one there give me place to sleep," he said sadly.

Pierre came up at that moment and said, "No doubt my fiddle is gone."

"Oh, no, it isn't," replied Philippe.

"But hasn't the Castle been plundered?"

"The fiddle, we hide it," said Red Bird.

"You lads hid my fiddle? But could it be safe anywhere in this Fort?"

"Come and see," said Red Bird.

"Come, Philippe," said Pierre.

"Am I allowed to leave?" Philippe asked.

They appealed to the guard and an English soldier was detailed to go with them.

Red Bird led the way toward the bake-house.

No baker was here, for he had been sent off with the rest to Oswego. The ovens were cold, as no bread had been baked for the last three days.

Suddenly, Red Bird was crawling into one of the ovens. The three others stood near the door and could see him wriggling along. In a few moments, he crawled out backwards, just as he had done when he had lighted the fire. He had something in his hand.

"My fiddle! Here she is!" exclaimed Pierre, as he took it.

"That was a good hiding place," said the soldier. "Clever lads to think of it."

"I thank you with all my heart," said Pierre. "My fiddle, she help me to pass many long winter evenings."

They returned to the chapel, where Captain Wentworth and Abbie were awaiting them. When Pierre had shown his fiddle and the Captain had praised the boys for taking such good care of it, Pierre turned to Red Bird and asked: "Red Bird, would you like to go with me? I teach you to be a voyageur. We will go up and down the rivers and the lakes together."

"Me like that," said Red Bird eagerly.

"We'll start soon," said Pierre. "Captain Wentworth will arrange for a guard to take us safe to the place where the Little Fort stood. There I get a canoe and we set out toward the west."

A half hour later they had gone, Philippe and Abbie waving good-by till they had disappeared through the Gate of the Five Nations.

The next morning a bateau was going east along the south shore of Lake Ontario, having just left the mouth of the great river Niagara. In it were Captain Wentworth, Abbie and Philippe, besides a guard of English soldiers and the canoe-men who were paddling. They were on their way to Oswego, to join the part of the English army returning to Albany.

It was a still, damp morning, with a light fog over the water. The great Fort lay quiet in the mist, as if no gun had ever sounded on its ramparts. The gray Castle stood safe and whole, in spite of the cannon balls that had battered its walls. The Lombardy poplars, stripped of a few limbs, still stood, overlooking the lake.

Through the misty air there came a dull sound from the southwest.

"What is that roar I keep hearing?" asked Captain Wentworth.

"The roar of the Falls," replied Abbie.

"Niagara Falls?" asked her father. "I would like to have seen that great wonder when I was so near. I suppose it is a marvelous sight."

"Oh, yes," said Philippe eagerly. "It is most grand and beautiful."

"I wish I had seen it, Father," said Abbie.

"I, too, wish you might have seen it, but the most important thing is to get you home as soon as possible. We are not entirely out of danger yet. Mother is anxiously watching for us, and we must not delay."

There was silence for a few minutes, as the swift strokes of the paddles sent the bateau on its way over the blue water.

One of the guard spoke, "Don't you think, Captain, that this capture of Fort Niagara is a great thing for the English?"

"Yes, since it guards the route to all the inland country. The fur trade will all come to us now," replied Captain Wentworth.

"Montreal and Quebec cannot hold out much longer."

"No; not with Niagara gone."

The strokes of the paddles sent the bateau swiftly forward. After half an hour the sun broke through the mist, flooding with golden light the peaceful lake, a happy omen of the new day dawning for Abbie and Philippe.

No longer are packs of furs carried down the Portage Road; no longer are canoes and their cargoes carried up that great Carrying-place; no longer do flotillas come into the mouth of the river; no longer do bands of Indians come to make treaties with belts of wampum.

The guns at Fort Niagara have long been silent. For over a hundred years two great nations have lived along the banks of the river in peace and good-will. Not only along the Niagara, but for a thousand leagues westward, the guns of the forts are stilled, and Canada and the United States live in friendship and peace.

But the great river goes on. Day and night, winter and summer, never does it pause in its rush to the sea. It gathers the waters from the

Great Lakes and carries them down through the rapids, where they swirl and leap and flash in the sunlight, and then go hurrying over the brink of the cataract with a deafening roar.

Always the river goes on, just as in the days of Red Bird, Pierre, Abbie and Philippe.

## THE END